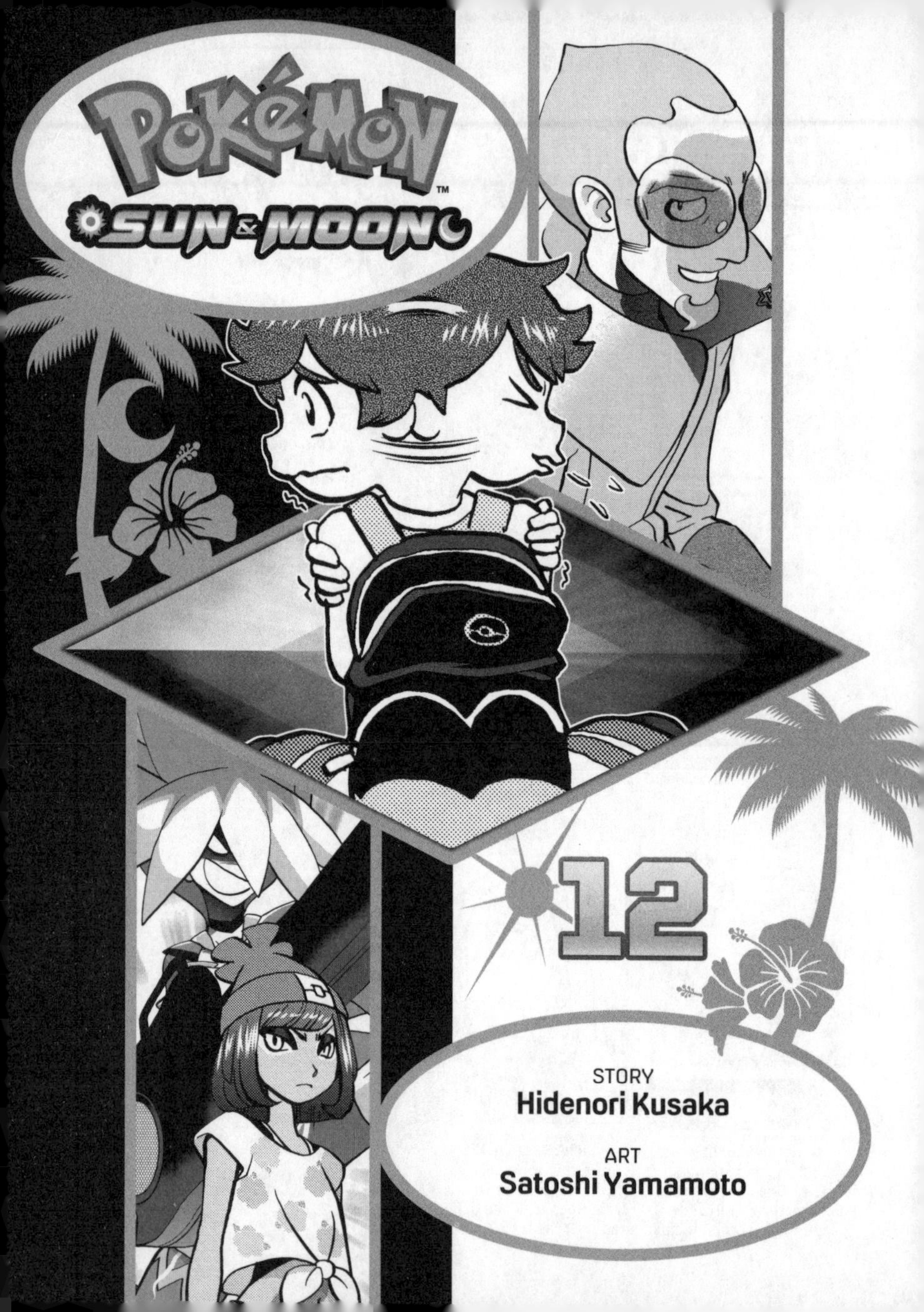
Pokémon™
SUN & MOON
12
STORY
Hidenori Kusaka
ART
Satoshi Yamamoto

Introduction

Sun

He was dragged into the Aether Foundation's scheme and disappeared into Ultra Space. It took him six months to escape.

Dollar (Torracat)

Cent (Alolan Meowth)

Quarter (Wishiwashi)

Penny (Mimikyu)

Loot (Crabominable)

Ray (Stakataka)

Moon

A pharmacist who has traveled to Alola from a faraway region. She is a self-confident, original thinker and an excellent archer.

Ultra Recon Squad

Mysterious people from another dimension who travel to Alola to conduct some sort of investigation.

Gladion

Lillie's brother. His partner is Silvally, a man-made Pokémon created specifically to fight against the Ultra Beasts!

Lillie

Lusamine's daughter and Gladion's timid younger sister. She has recently learned the importance of depending on other people.

Character

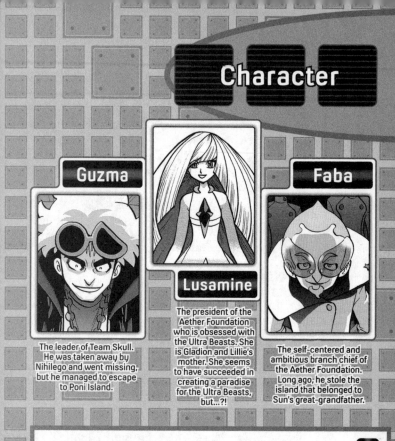

Guzma

The leader of Team Skull. He was taken away by Nihilego and went missing, but he managed to escape to Poni Island.

Lusamine

The president of the Aether Foundation who is obsessed with the Ultra Beasts. She is Gladion and Lillie's mother. She seems to have succeeded in creating a paradise for the Ultra Beasts, but...?!

Faba

The self-centered and ambitious branch chief of the Aether Foundation. Long ago, he stole the island that belonged to Sun's great-grandfather.

The Story Thus Far...

Moon, a pharmacist from another region, comes to the flower-filled vacation paradise of the Alola region, which consists of numerous tropical islands. While on an important errand, Moon meets Sun, who works various odd jobs and runs a delivery service to reach his goal of saving up a million dollars. When the Island Guardians of the Alolan Islands, called Tapu, become agitated, Sun is chosen to complete the island challenge to soothe the Tapus' anger. Moon comes along to help. Sun successfully completes the challenge by delivering a special Berry to the Tapu on different islands. While on the island of Poni, Sun and Moon play the legendary Sun and Moon flutes, causing two Cosmoem to transform into Solgaleo, the emissary of sun, and Lunala, the emissary of the moon! Sun and Moon are sucked into the crack in the sky and find themselves in a mysterious world called Ultra Space, where they meet Lusamine, president of the Aether Foundation, who has been possessed by Nihilego! Moon tries to free Lusamine by capturing Nihilego! She shoots an arrow toward Lusamine as a bright light illuminates the sky.

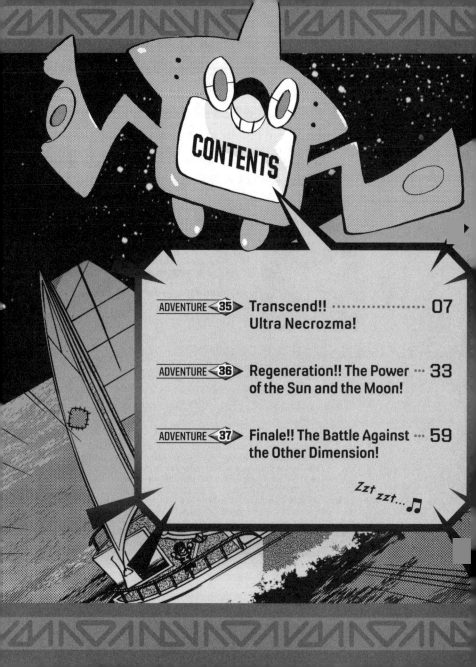

CONTENTS

Zzt zzt...♪

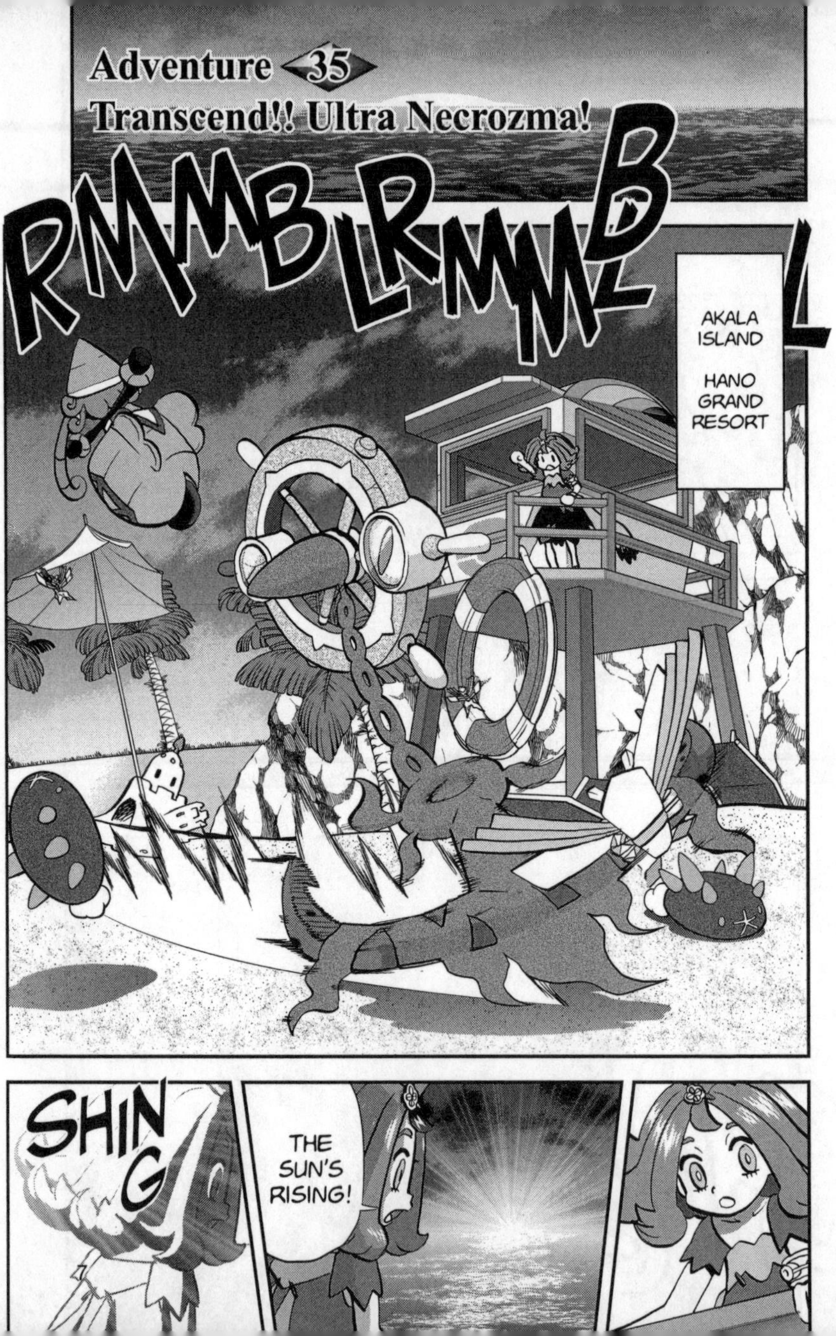
Adventure 35
Transcend!! Ultra Necrozma!
RMMBLRMMBL
AKALA ISLAND
HANO GRAND RESORT
THE SUN'S RISING!
SHING

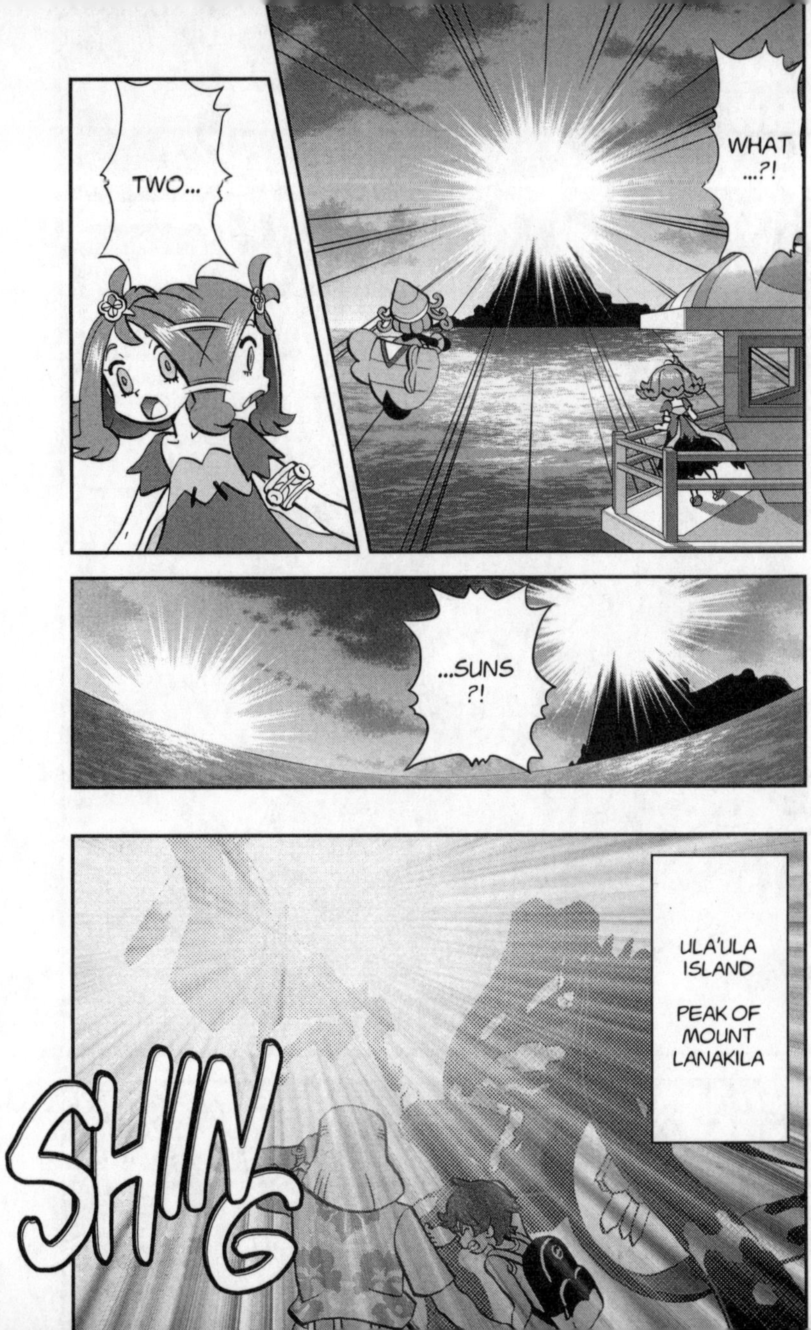
WHAT ...?!
TWO...
...SUNS ?!
ULA'ULA ISLAND
PEAK OF MOUNT LANAKILA
SHING

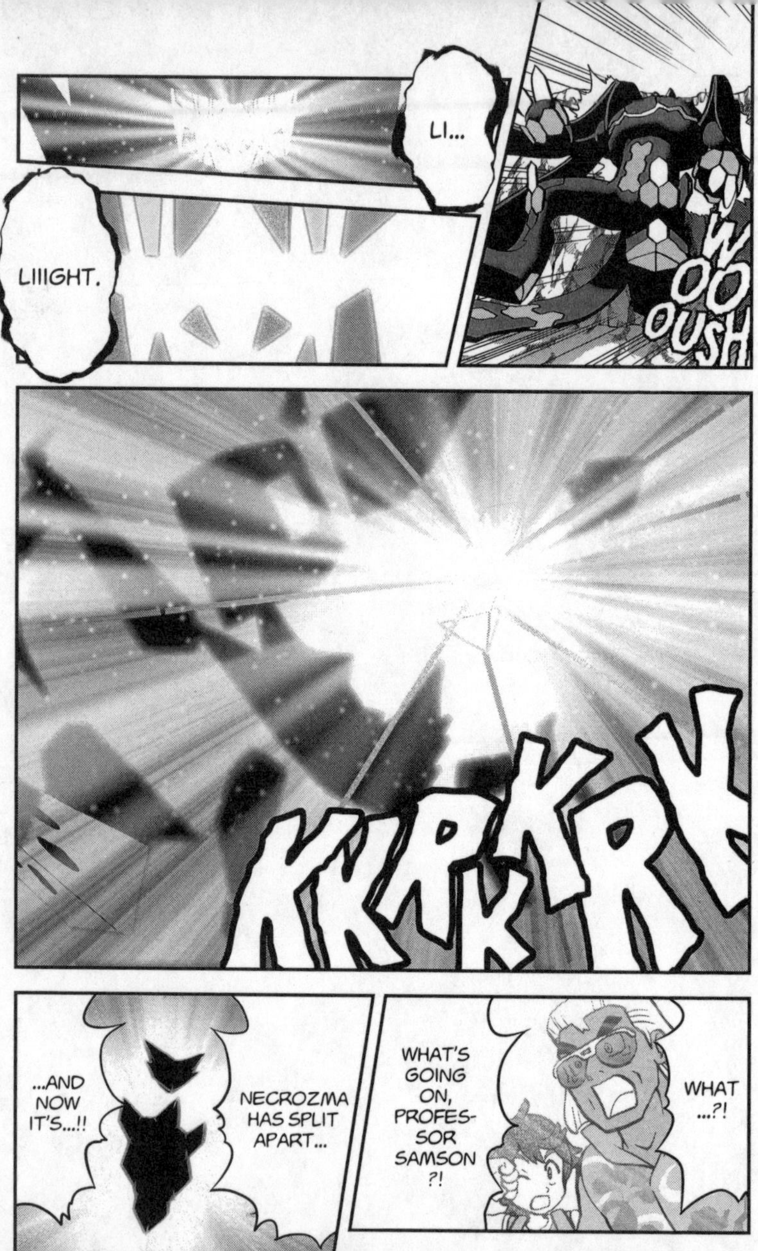
WOOOUSH
LI...
LIIIGHT.
KKRKKRK
WHAT ...?!
WHAT'S GOING ON, PROFES-SOR SAMSON ?!
NECROZMA HAS SPLIT APART...
...AND NOW IT'S...!!

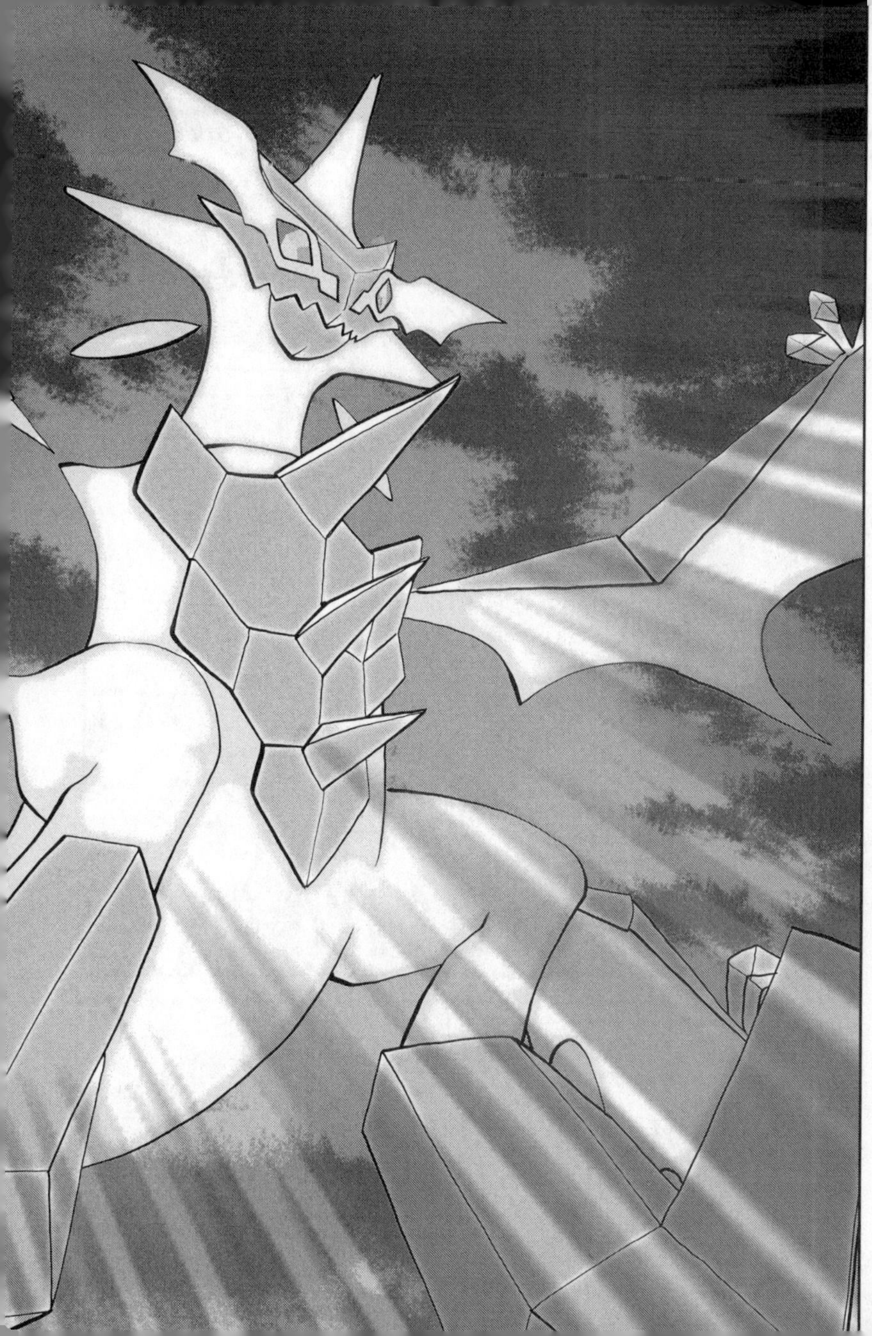

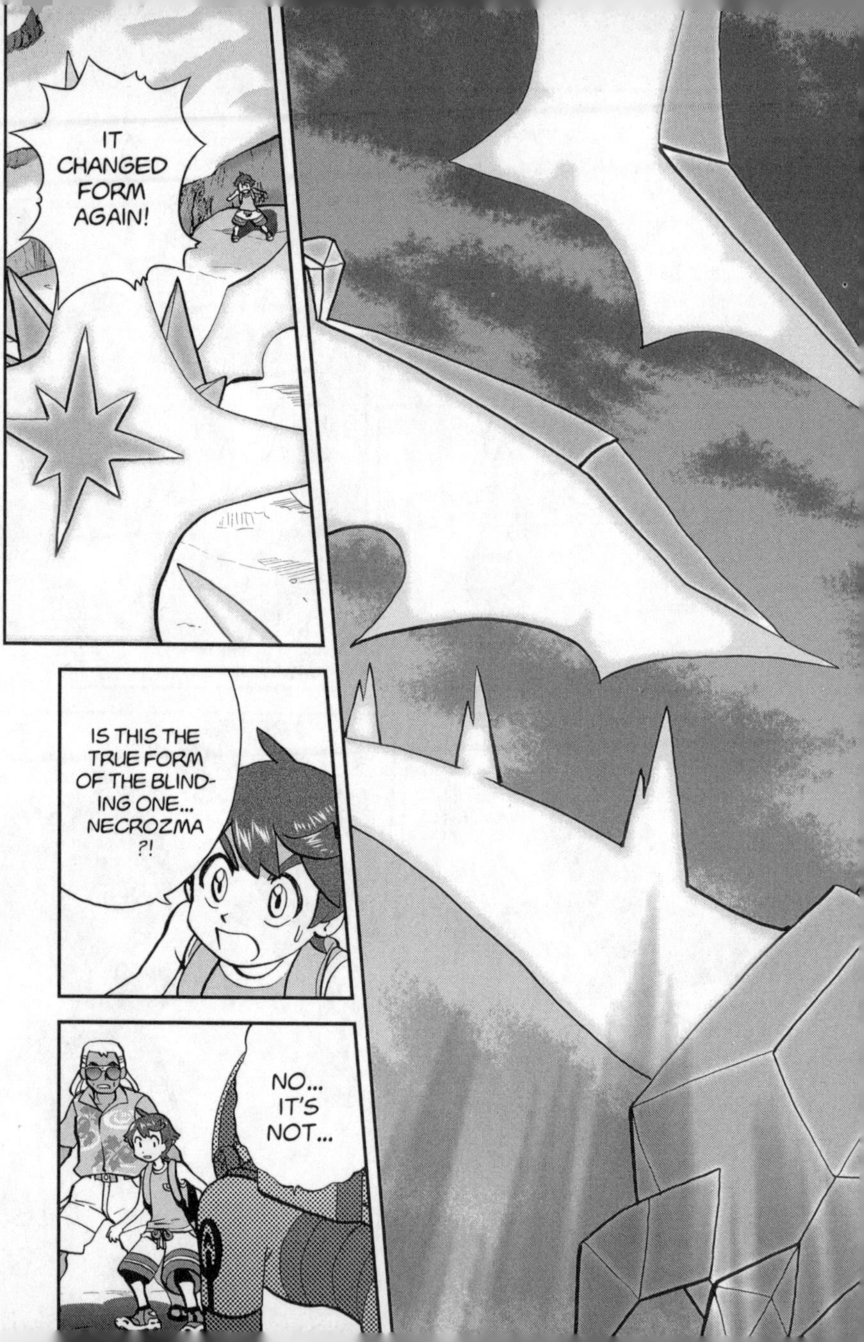
IT CHANGED FORM AGAIN!
IS THIS THE TRUE FORM OF THE BLINDING ONE... NECROZMA ?!
NO... IT'S NOT...

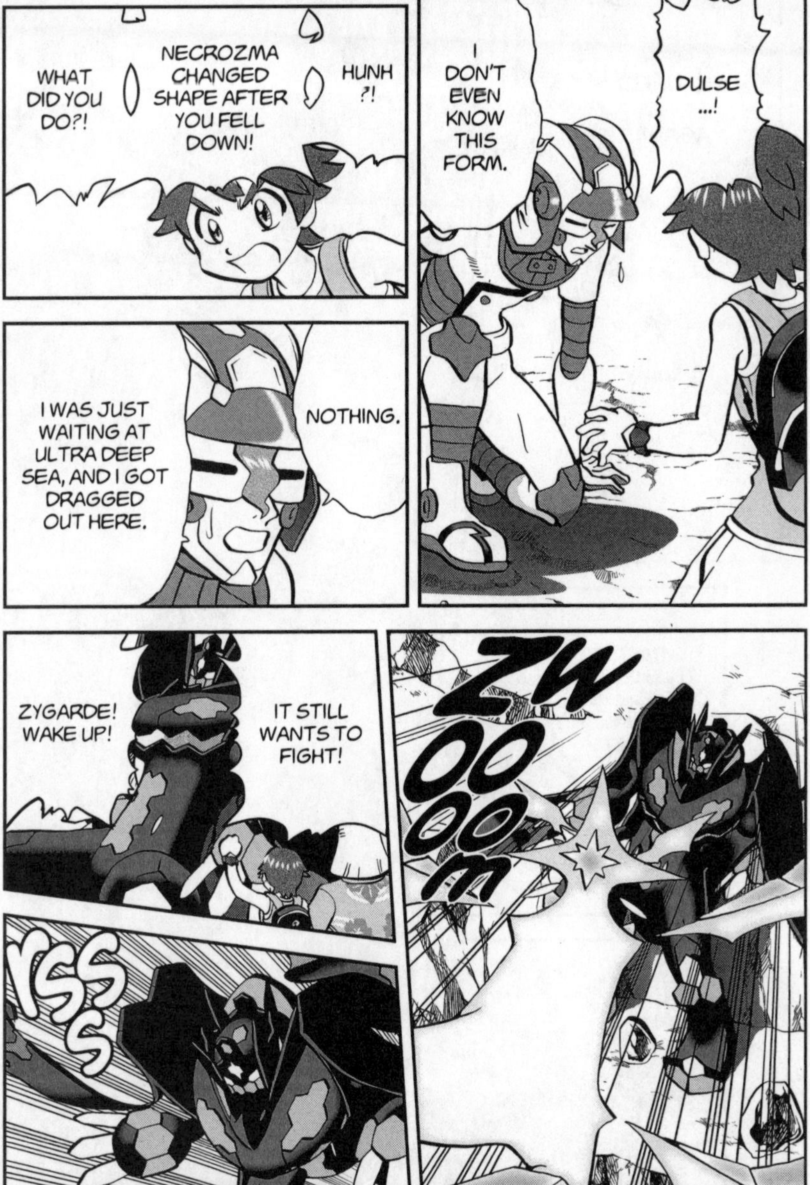
DULSE ...!
I DON'T EVEN KNOW THIS FORM.
HUNH ?!
NECROZMA CHANGED SHAPE AFTER YOU FELL DOWN!
WHAT DID YOU DO?!
NOTHING.
I WAS JUST WAITING AT ULTRA DEEP SEA, AND I GOT DRAGGED OUT HERE.
ZWOOOOM
IT STILL WANTS TO FIGHT!
ZYGARDE! WAKE UP!

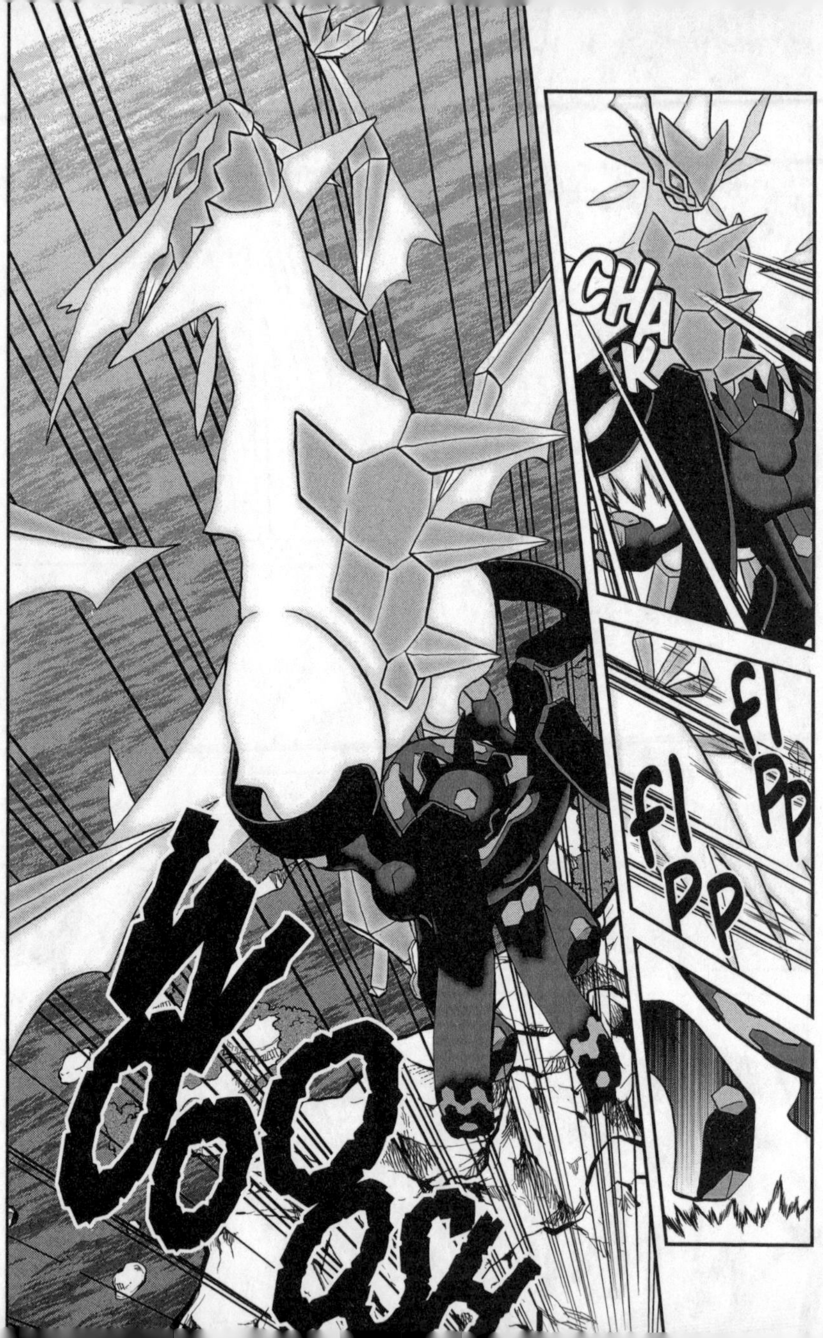
CHAK
flipp flipp
WOOOSH

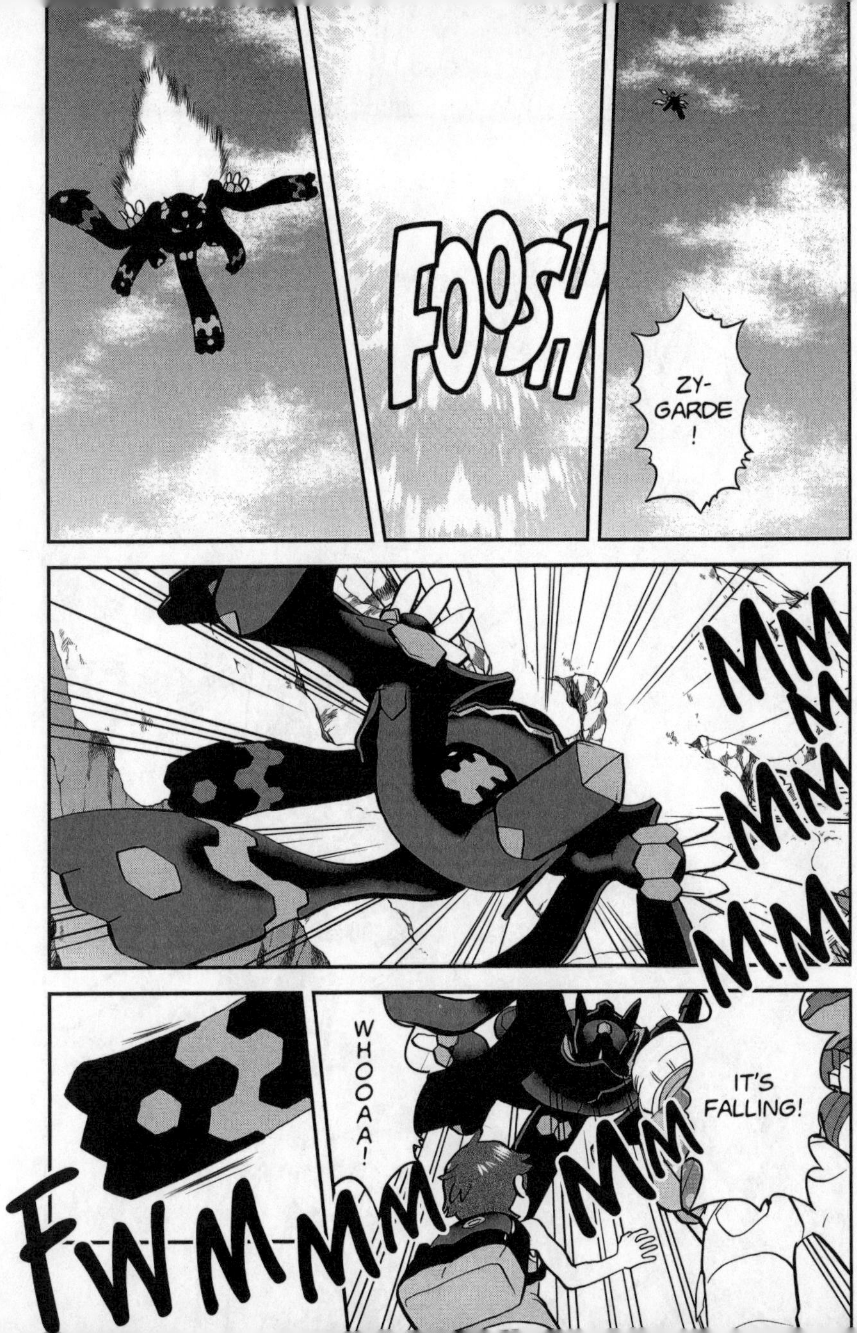
ZY-GARDE!
FOOSH
MMMMMMMMMMM
IT'S FALLING!
WHOOAAA!
FWMMMMMMM

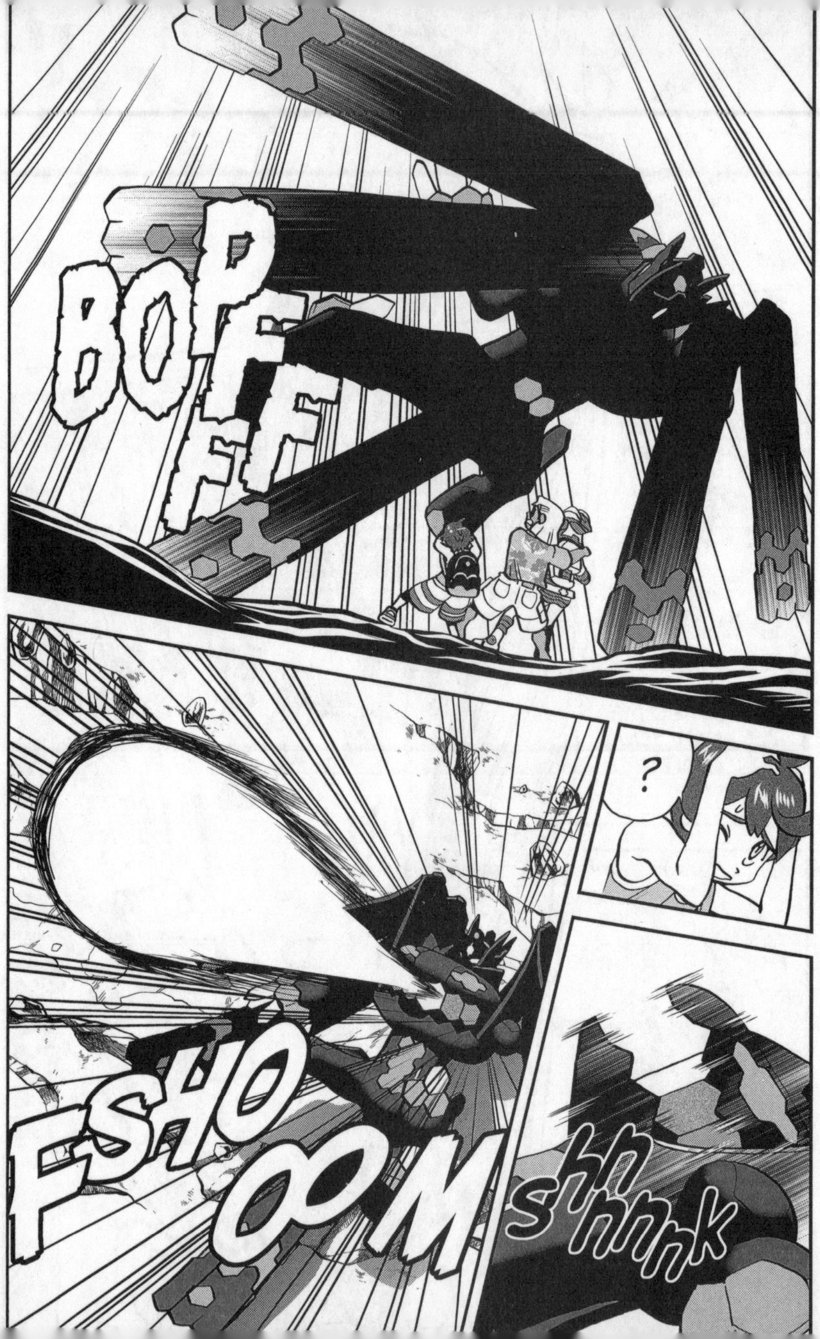
BOPFF
?
FSHOOOM
shhhnk

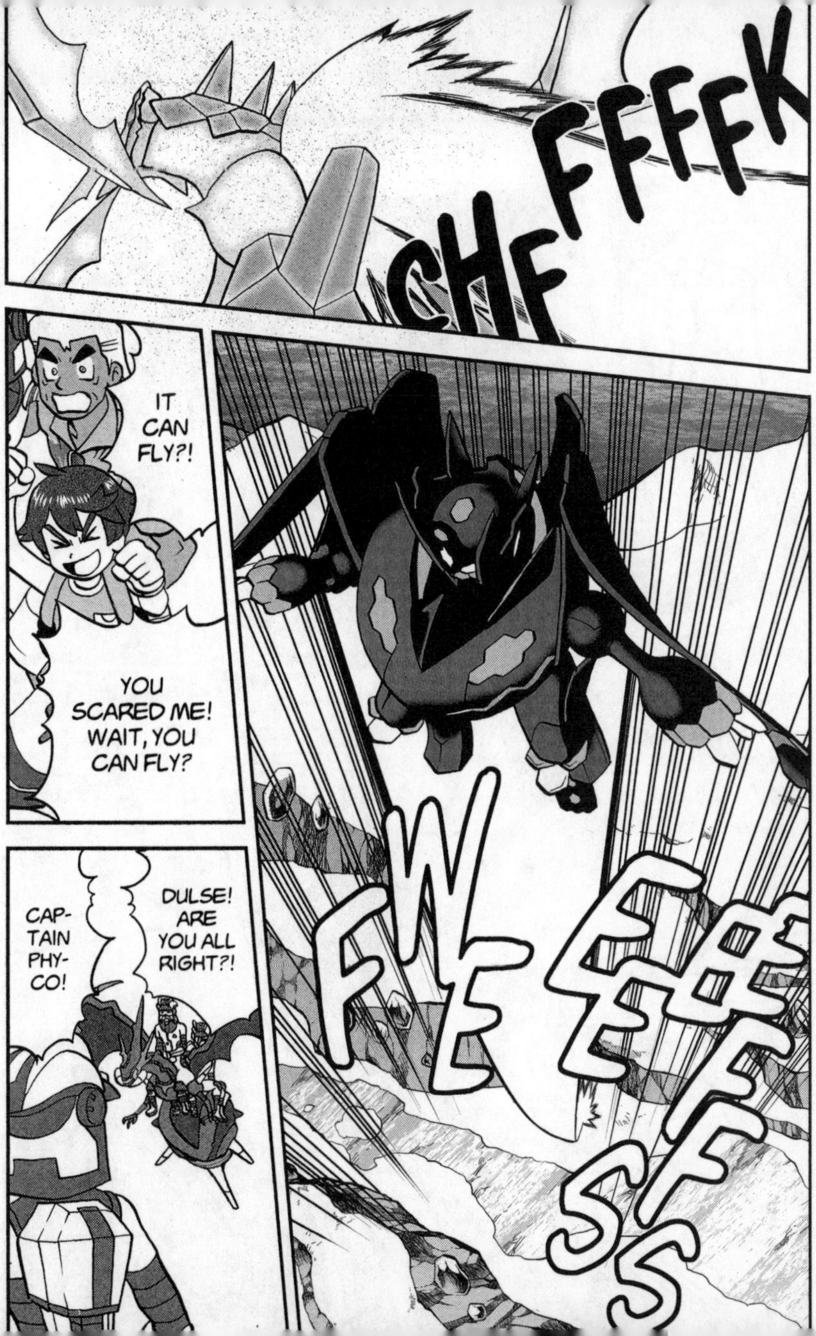
CHFFFFK
IT CAN FLY?!
YOU SCARED ME! WAIT, YOU CAN FLY?
DULSE! ARE YOU ALL RIGHT?!
CAP-TAIN PHY-CO!

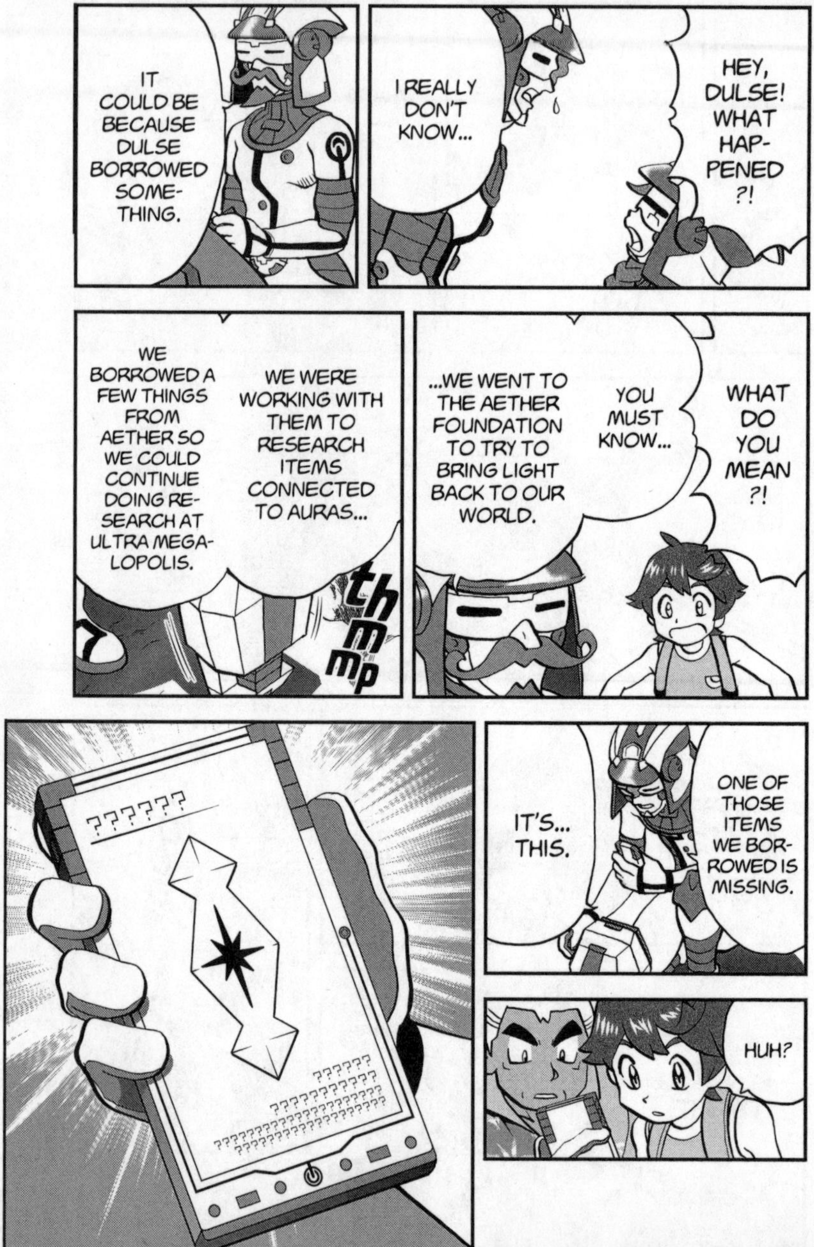
HEY, DULSE! WHAT HAP-PENED?!
I REALLY DON'T KNOW...
IT COULD BE BECAUSE DULSE BORROWED SOME-THING.
WHAT DO YOU MEAN?!
YOU MUST KNOW...
...WE WENT TO THE AETHER FOUNDATION TO TRY TO BRING LIGHT BACK TO OUR WORLD.
WE WERE WORKING WITH THEM TO RESEARCH ITEMS CONNECTED TO AURAS...
WE BORROWED A FEW THINGS FROM AETHER SO WE COULD CONTINUE DOING RE-SEARCH AT ULTRA MEGA-LOPOLIS.
thmmp
ONE OF THOSE ITEMS WE BOR-ROWED IS MISSING.
IT'S... THIS.
HUH?
??????

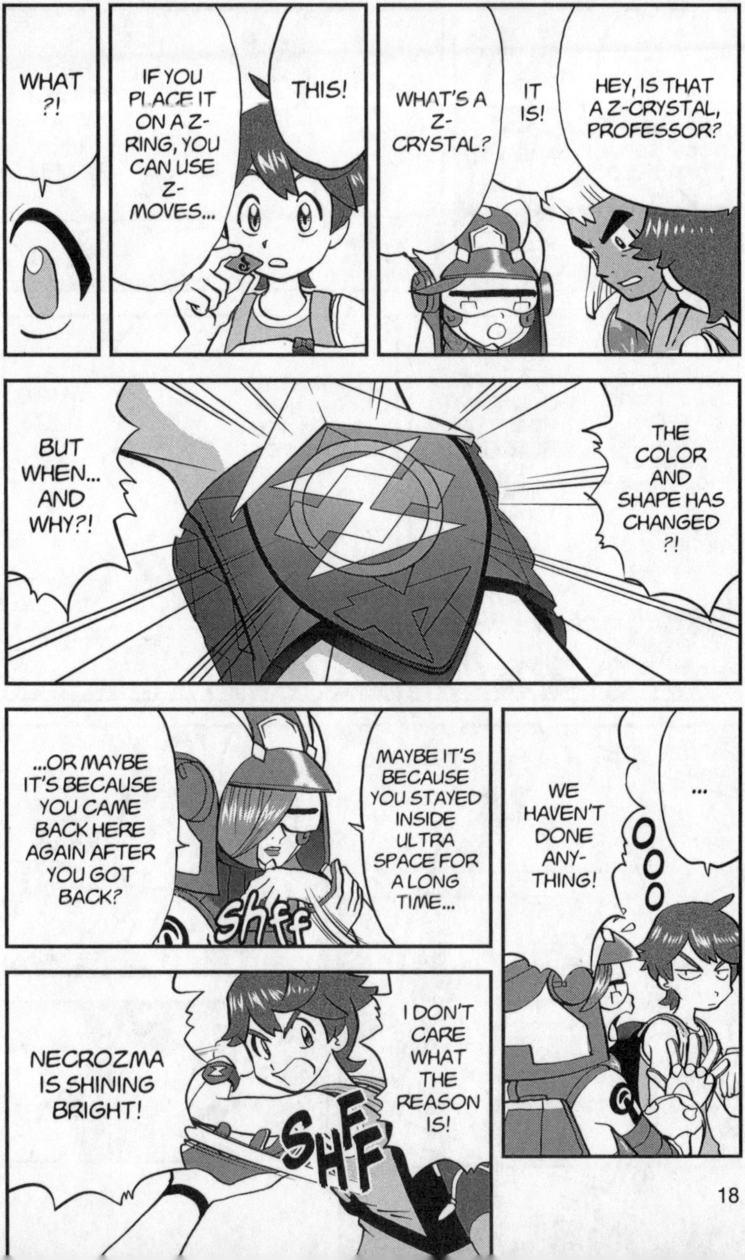
HEY, IS THAT A Z-CRYSTAL, PROFESSOR?
IT IS!
WHAT'S A Z-CRYSTAL?
THIS!
IF YOU PLACE IT ON A Z-RING, YOU CAN USE Z-MOVES...
WHAT?!
THE COLOR AND SHAPE HAS CHANGED?!
BUT WHEN... AND WHY?!
...
WE HAVEN'T DONE ANYTHING!
OOO
MAYBE IT'S BECAUSE YOU STAYED INSIDE ULTRA SPACE FOR A LONG TIME...
...OR MAYBE IT'S BECAUSE YOU CAME BACK HERE AGAIN AFTER YOU GOT BACK?
shff
I DON'T CARE WHAT THE REASON IS!
NECROZMA IS SHINING BRIGHT!
SHFF

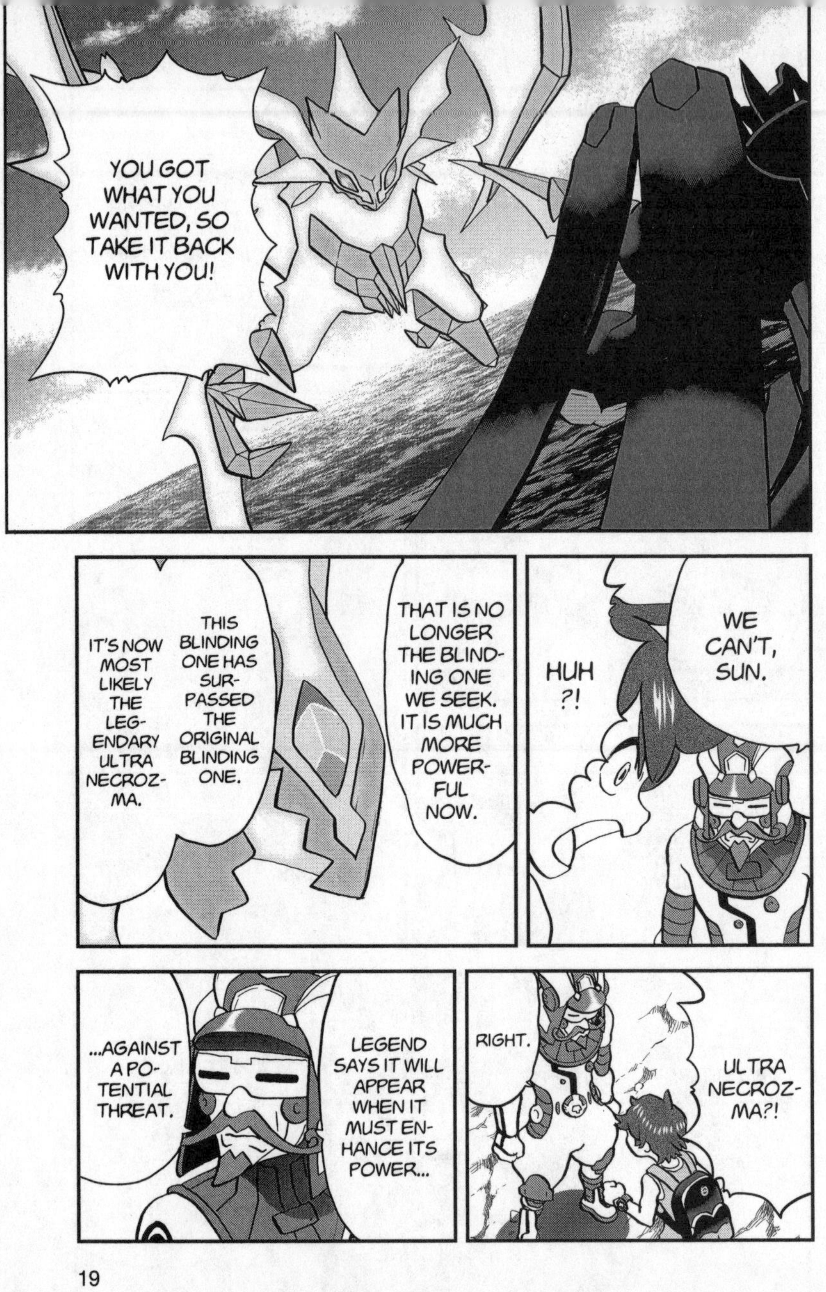
YOU GOT WHAT YOU WANTED, SO TAKE IT BACK WITH YOU!
WE CAN'T, SUN.
HUH ?!
THAT IS NO LONGER THE BLINDING ONE WE SEEK. IT IS MUCH MORE POWERFUL NOW.
THIS BLINDING ONE HAS SURPASSED THE ORIGINAL BLINDING ONE.
IT'S NOW MOST LIKELY THE LEGENDARY ULTRA NECROZMA.
ULTRA NECROZMA?!
RIGHT.
LEGEND SAYS IT WILL APPEAR WHEN IT MUST ENHANCE ITS POWER...
...AGAINST A POTENTIAL THREAT.

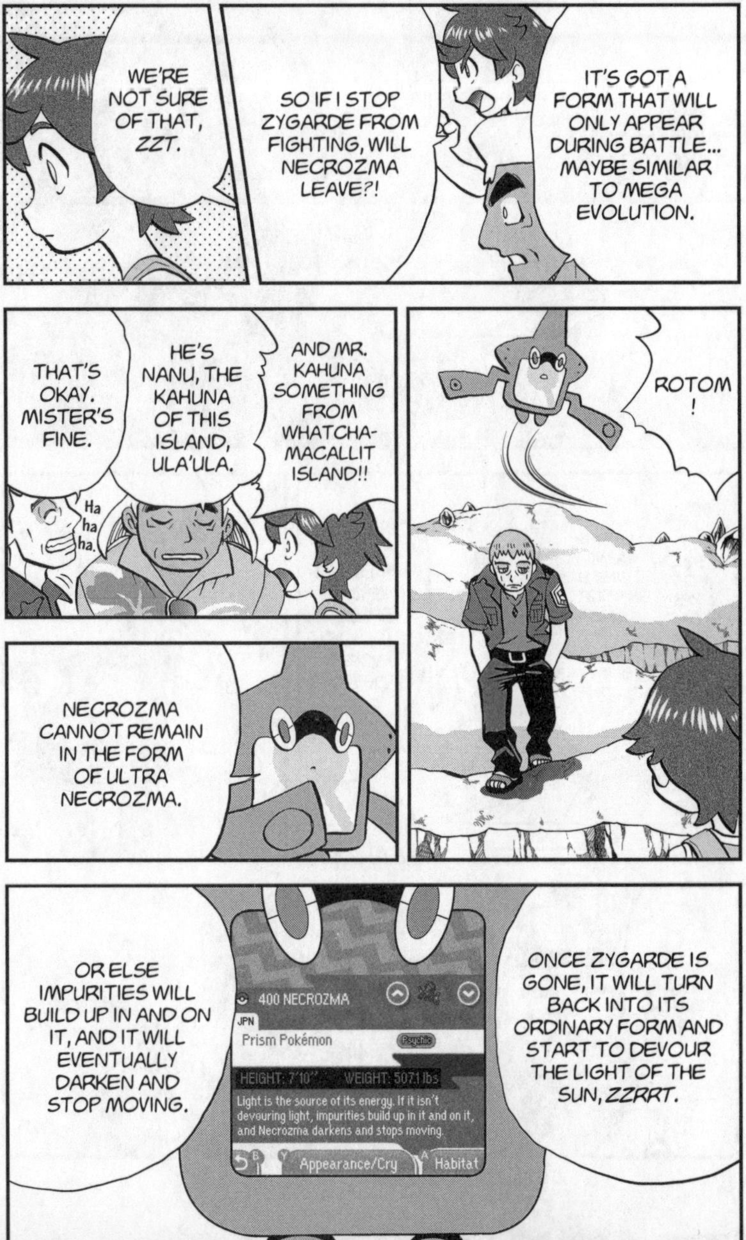
IT'S GOT A FORM THAT WILL ONLY APPEAR DURING BATTLE... MAYBE SIMILAR TO MEGA EVOLUTION.
SO IF I STOP ZYGARDE FROM FIGHTING, WILL NECROZMA LEAVE?!
WE'RE NOT SURE OF THAT, ZZT.
ROTOM!
AND MR. KAHUNA SOMETHING FROM WHATCHA-MACALLIT ISLAND!!
HE'S NANU, THE KAHUNA OF THIS ISLAND, ULA'ULA.
Ha ha ha.
THAT'S OKAY. MISTER'S FINE.
NECROZMA CANNOT REMAIN IN THE FORM OF ULTRA NECROZMA.
ONCE ZYGARDE IS GONE, IT WILL TURN BACK INTO ITS ORDINARY FORM AND START TO DEVOUR THE LIGHT OF THE SUN, ZZRRT.
400 NECROZMA
JPN
Prism Pokémon
Psychic
HEIGHT: 7'10" WEIGHT: 507.1 lbs
Light is the source of its energy. If it isn't devouring light, impurities build up in it and on it, and Necrozma darkens and stops moving.
Appearance/Cry
Habitat
OR ELSE IMPURITIES WILL BUILD UP IN AND ON IT, AND IT WILL EVENTUALLY DARKEN AND STOP MOVING.

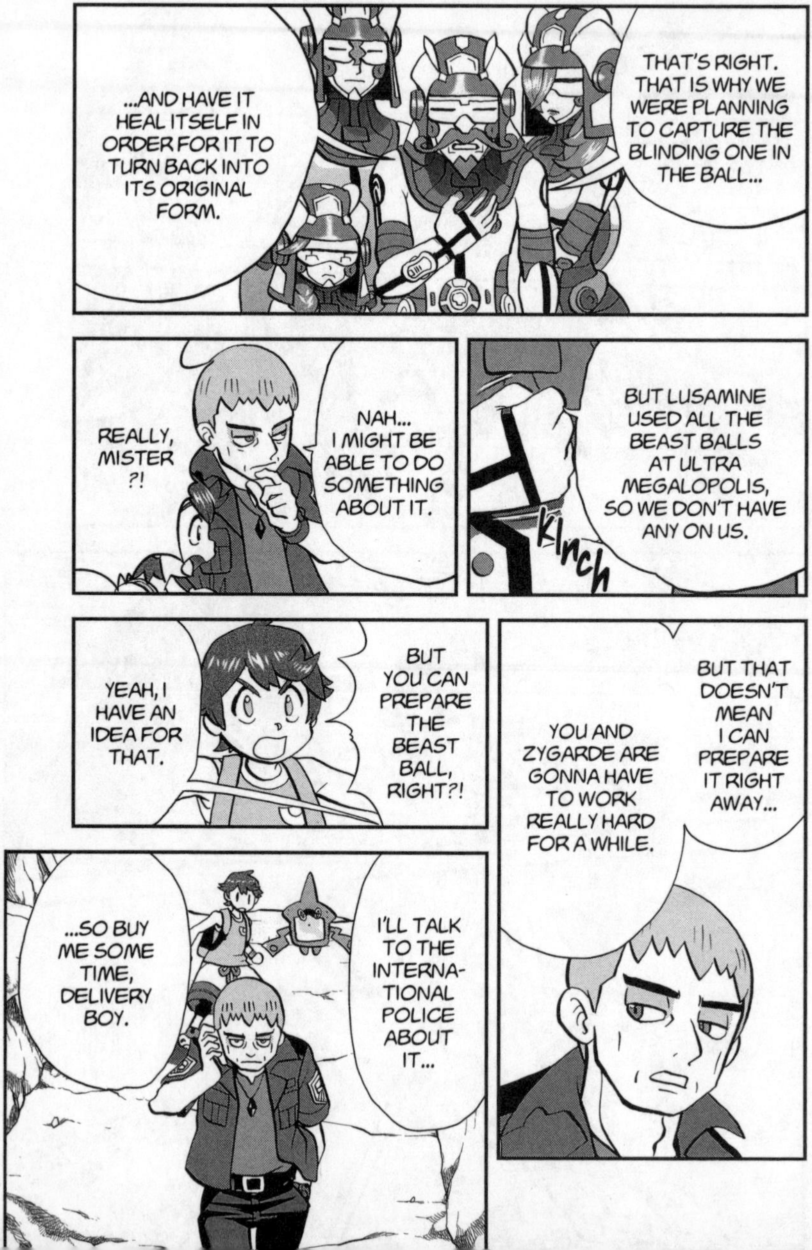
THAT'S RIGHT. THAT IS WHY WE WERE PLANNING TO CAPTURE THE BLINDING ONE IN THE BALL...
...AND HAVE IT HEAL ITSELF IN ORDER FOR IT TO TURN BACK INTO ITS ORIGINAL FORM.
BUT LUSAMINE USED ALL THE BEAST BALLS AT ULTRA MEGALOPOLIS, SO WE DON'T HAVE ANY ON US.
KLRCH
NAH... I MIGHT BE ABLE TO DO SOMETHING ABOUT IT.
REALLY, MISTER ?!
BUT THAT DOESN'T MEAN I CAN PREPARE IT RIGHT AWAY...
YOU AND ZYGARDE ARE GONNA HAVE TO WORK REALLY HARD FOR A WHILE.
BUT YOU CAN PREPARE THE BEAST BALL, RIGHT?!
YEAH, I HAVE AN IDEA FOR THAT.
I'LL TALK TO THE INTERNA-TIONAL POLICE ABOUT IT...
...SO BUY ME SOME TIME, DELIVERY BOY.

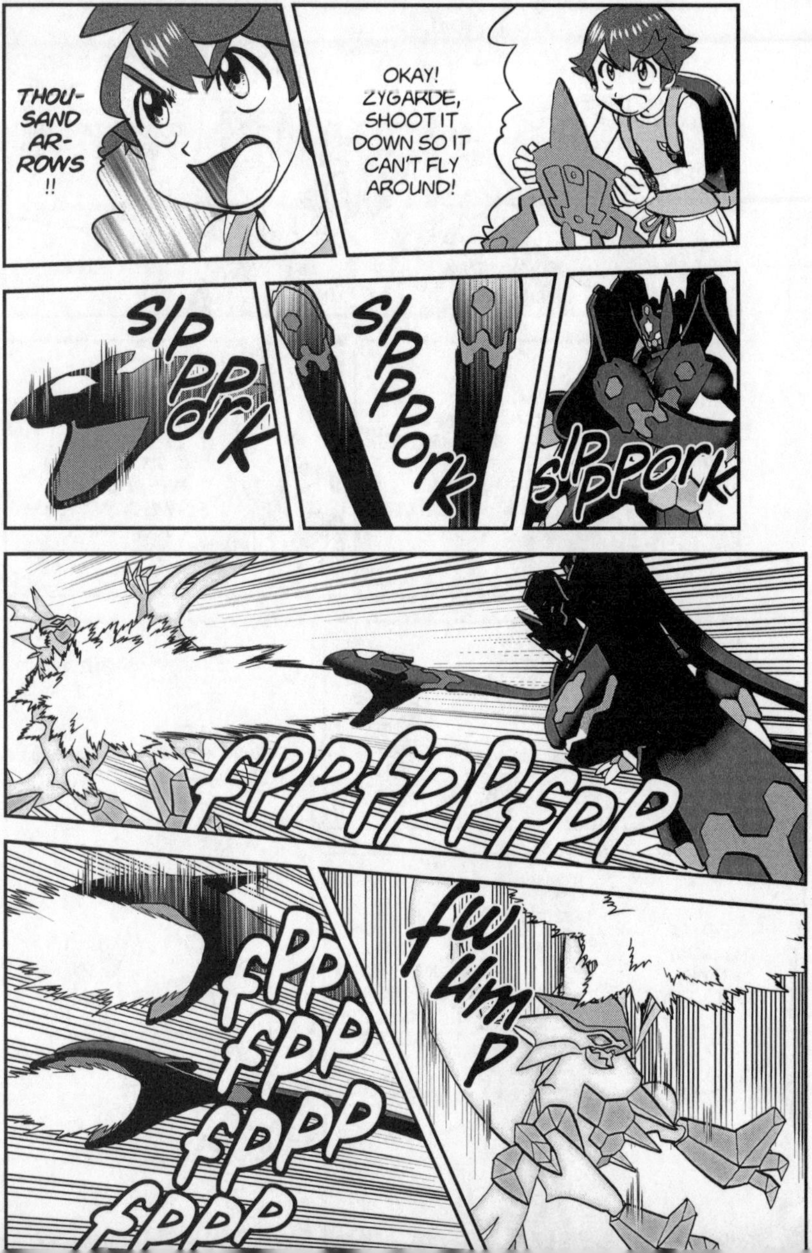
OKAY! ZYGARDE, SHOOT IT DOWN SO IT CAN'T FLY AROUND!
THOU-SAND AR-ROWS!!
slppork
slpppork
slppork
fppfppfpp
fwump
fpp fpp fppp fppp

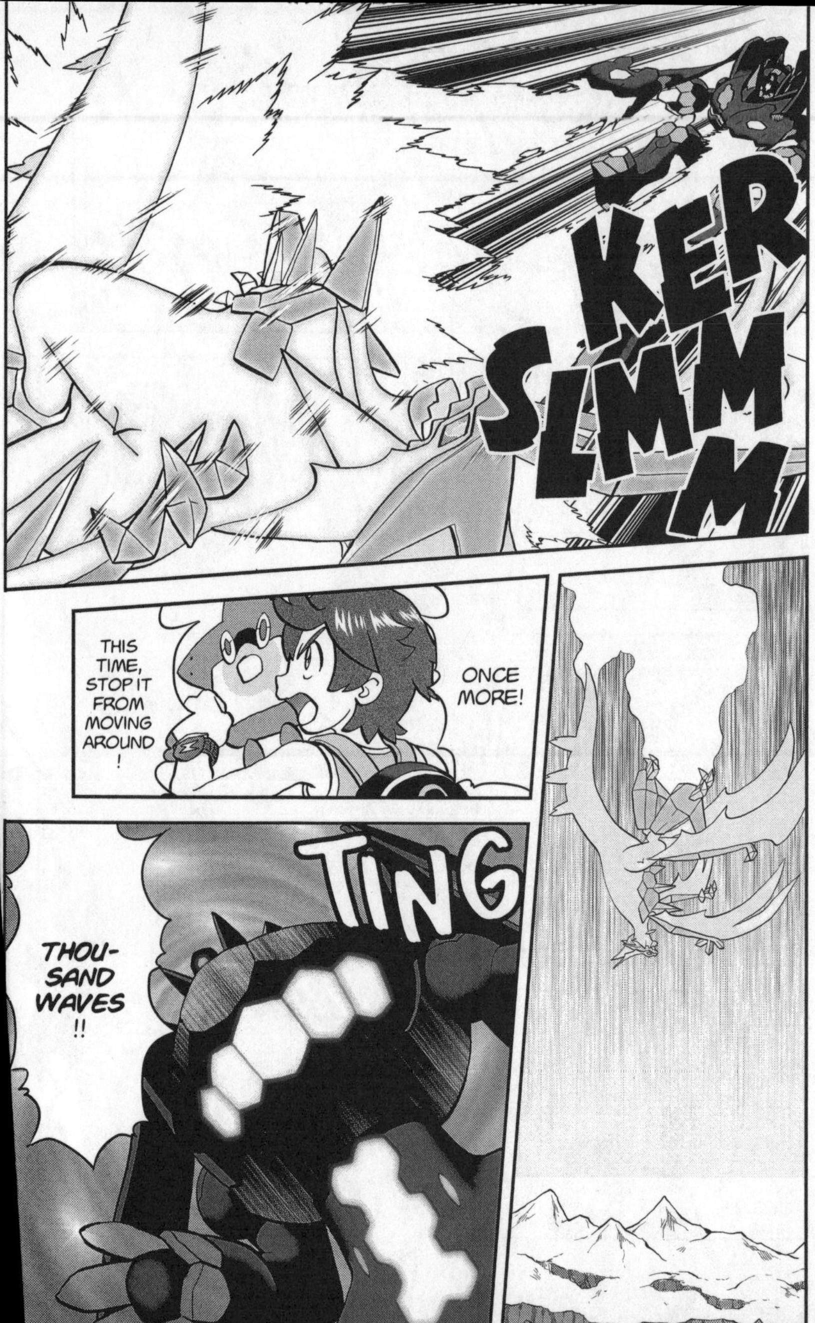
KER
SLMMM
ONCE MORE!
THIS TIME, STOP IT FROM MOVING AROUND!
TING
THOU-SAND WAVES!!

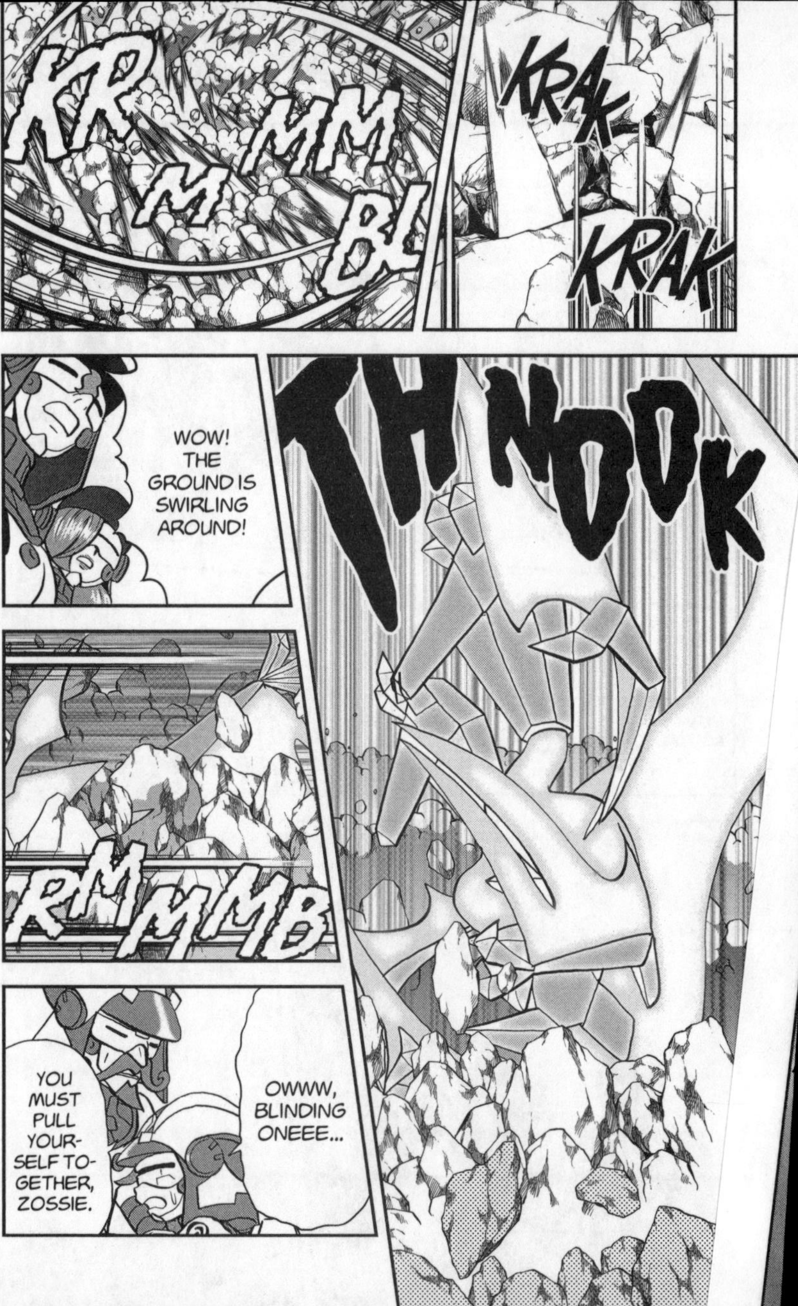
KRAK
KRAK
KRMMMBL
THNOOK
WOW! THE GROUND IS SWIRLING AROUND!
RMMMB
OWWW, BLINDING ONEEE...
YOU MUST PULL YOURSELF TOGETHER, ZOSSIE.

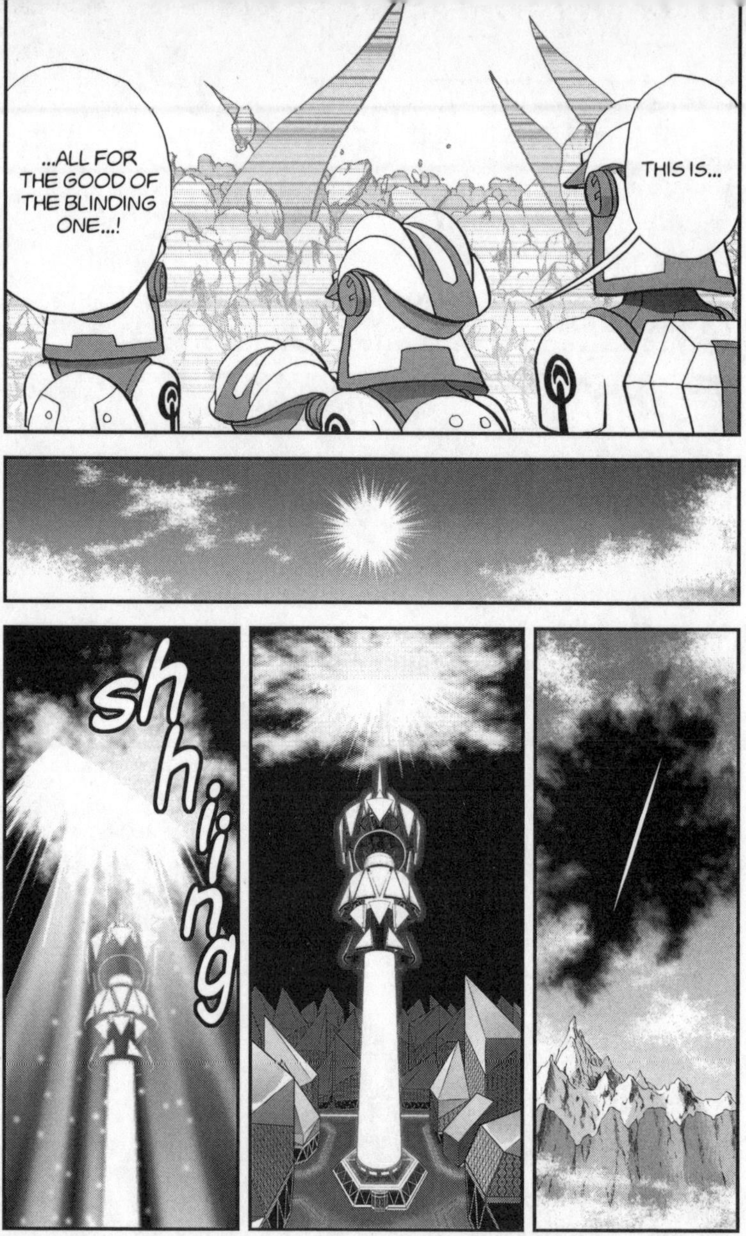
THIS IS...
...ALL FOR THE GOOD OF THE BLINDING ONE...!
shhiiing

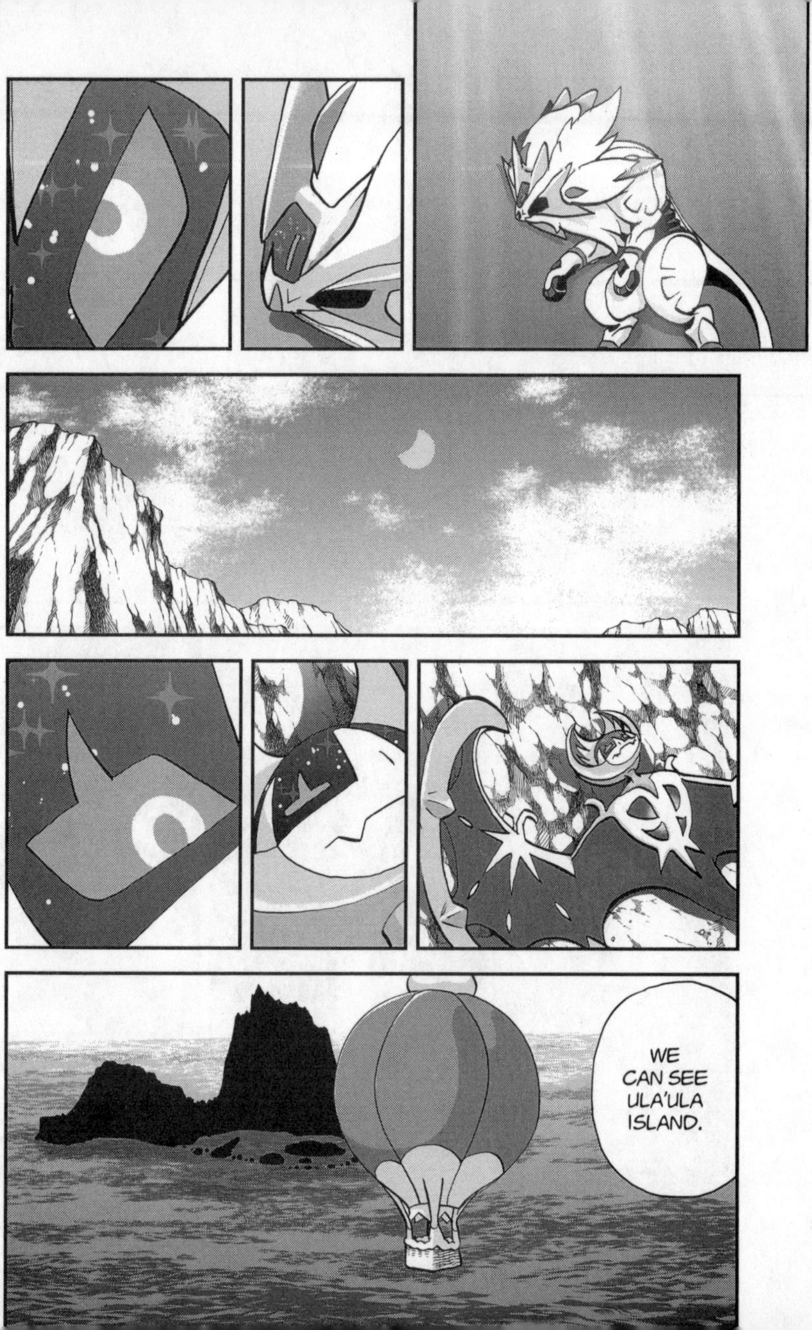
WE CAN SEE ULA'ULA ISLAND.

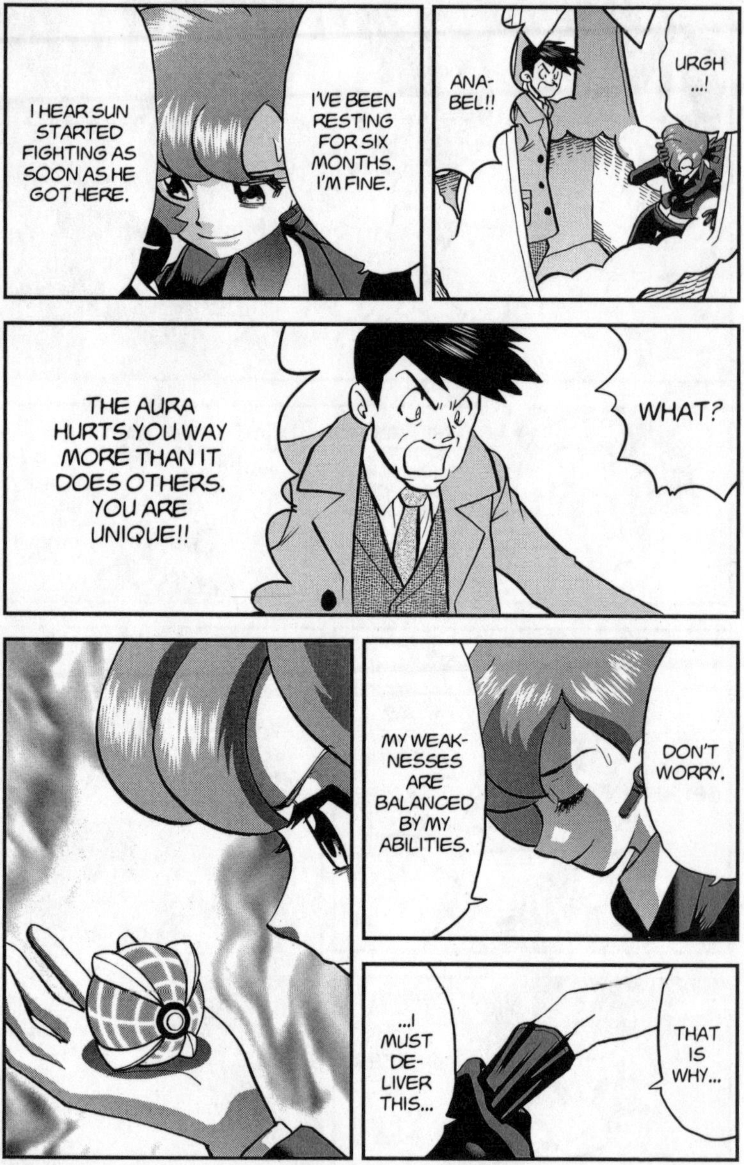
URGH ...!
ANA-BEL!!
I'VE BEEN RESTING FOR SIX MONTHS. I'M FINE.
I HEAR SUN STARTED FIGHTING AS SOON AS HE GOT HERE.
WHAT?
THE AURA HURTS YOU WAY MORE THAN IT DOES OTHERS. YOU ARE UNIQUE!!
DON'T WORRY.
MY WEAK-NESSES ARE BALANCED BY MY ABILITIES.
THAT IS WHY...
...I MUST DE-LIVER THIS...

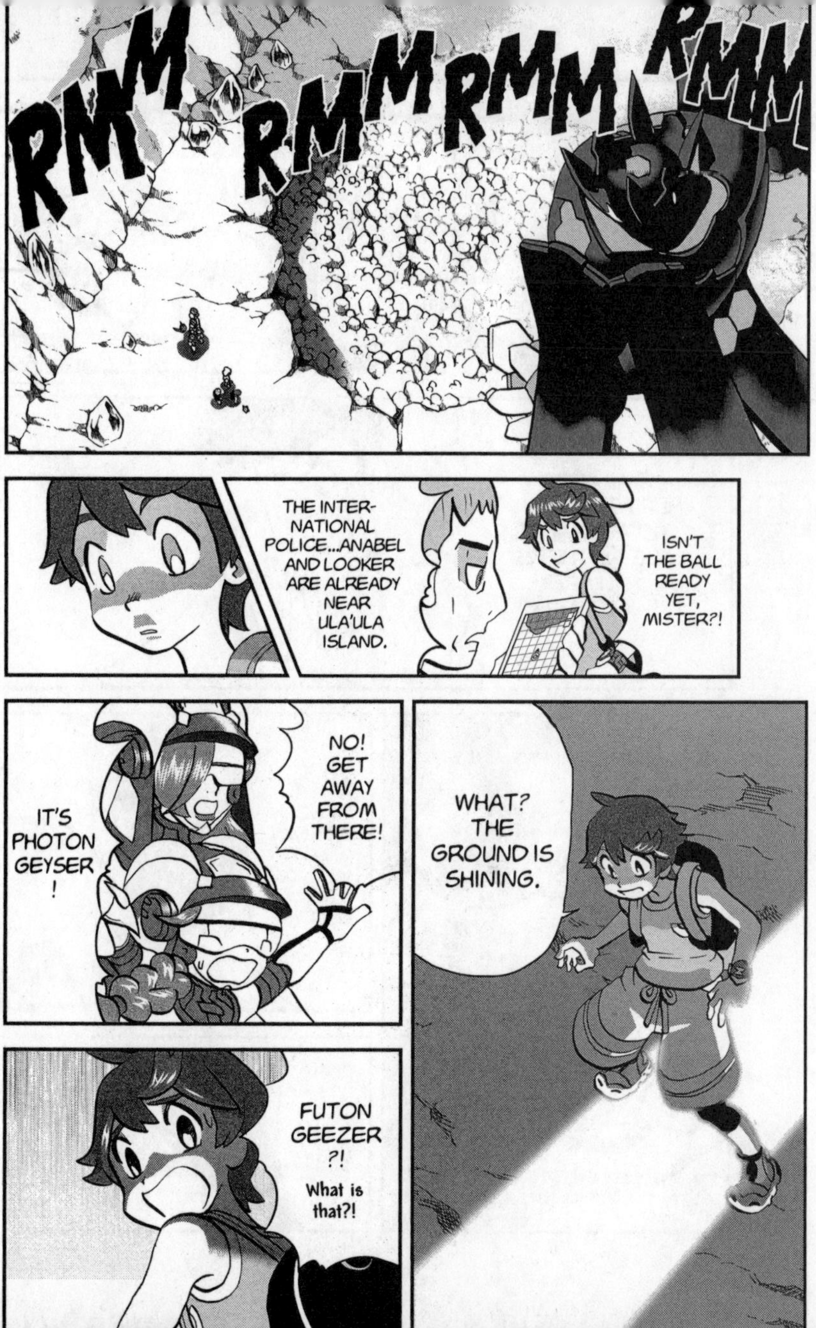
RMM
RMM
RMM
RMM
RMM
ISN'T THE BALL READY YET, MISTER?!
THE INTER-NATIONAL POLICE...ANABEL AND LOOKER ARE ALREADY NEAR ULA'ULA ISLAND.
WHAT? THE GROUND IS SHINING.
NO! GET AWAY FROM THERE!
IT'S PHOTON GEYSER!
FUTON GEEZER?!
What is that?!

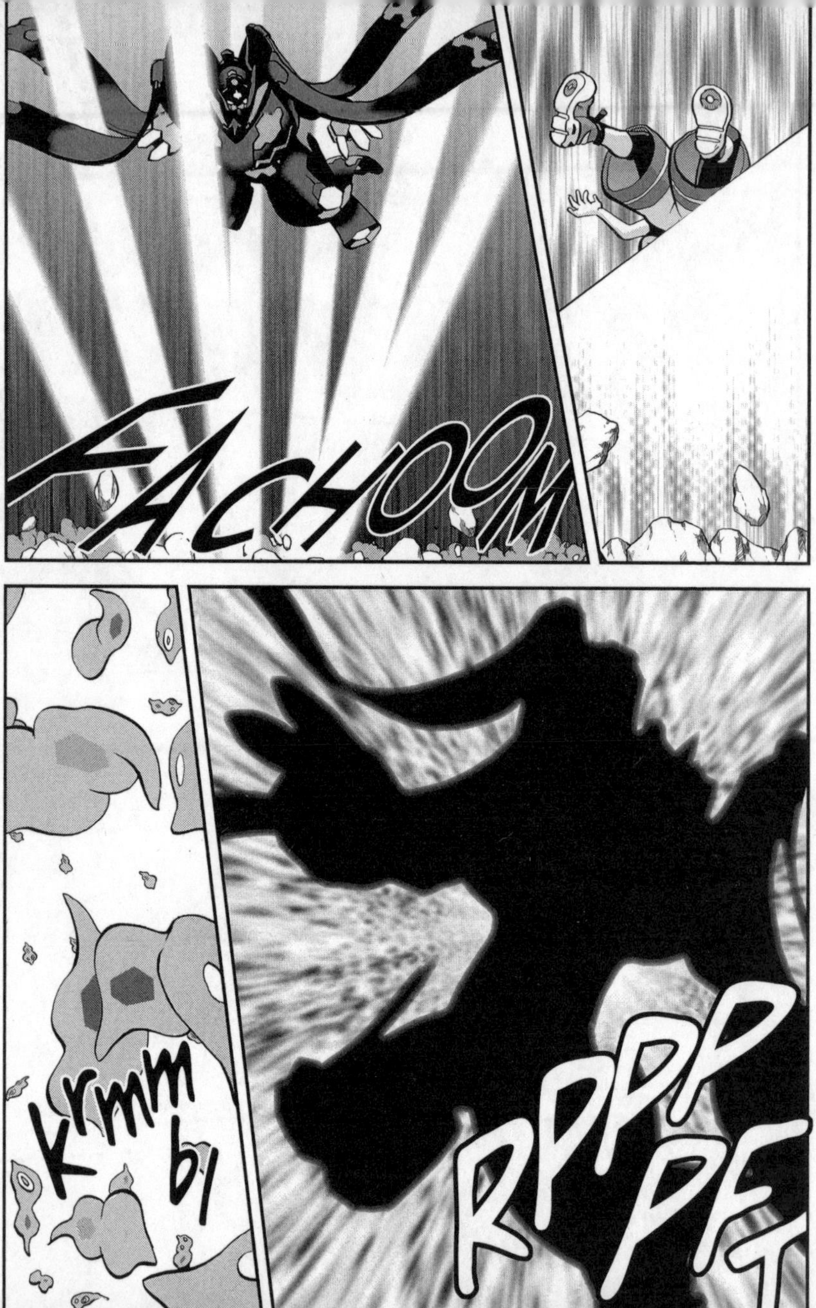
FACHOOM
RPPPPFT
krmm bl

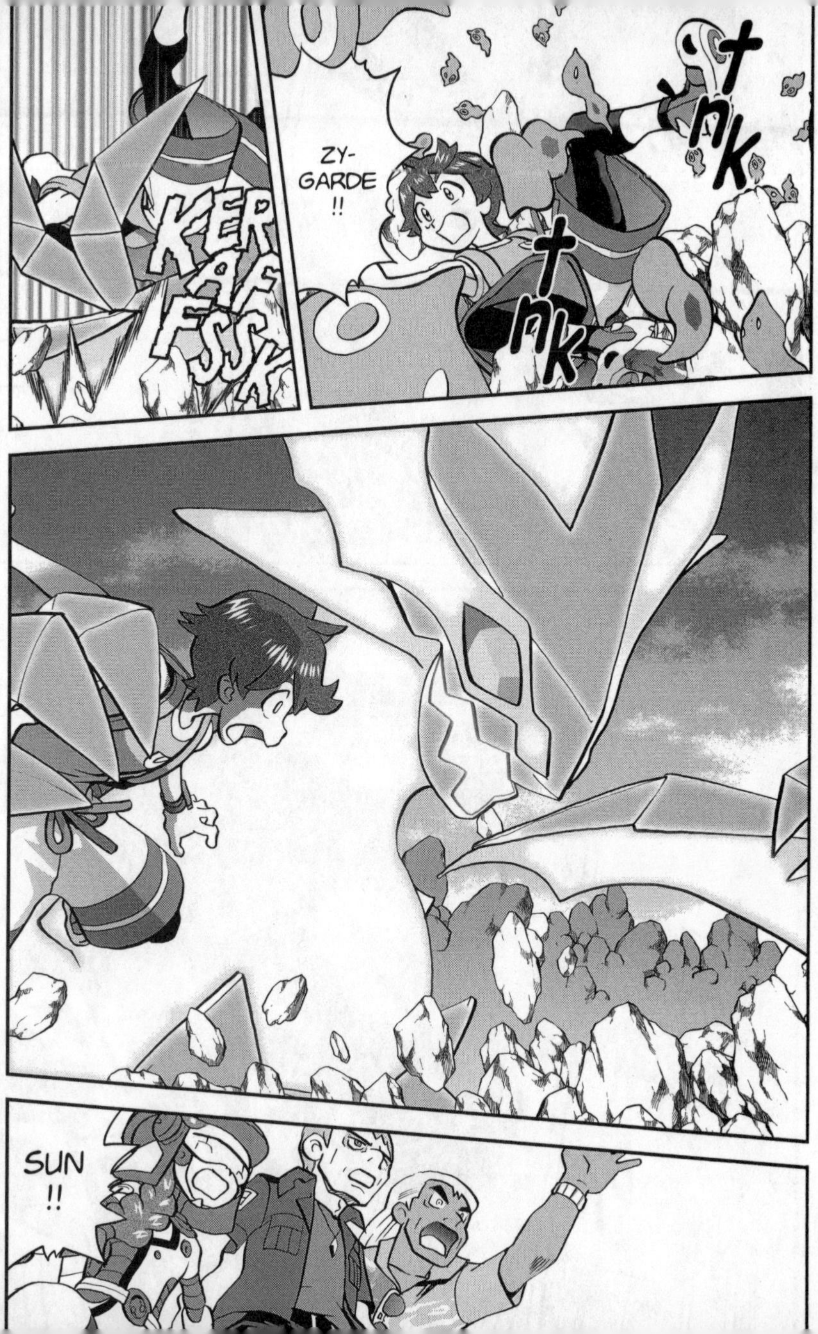
tnk
tnk
ZY-GARDE !!
KERAFFSSK
SUN !!

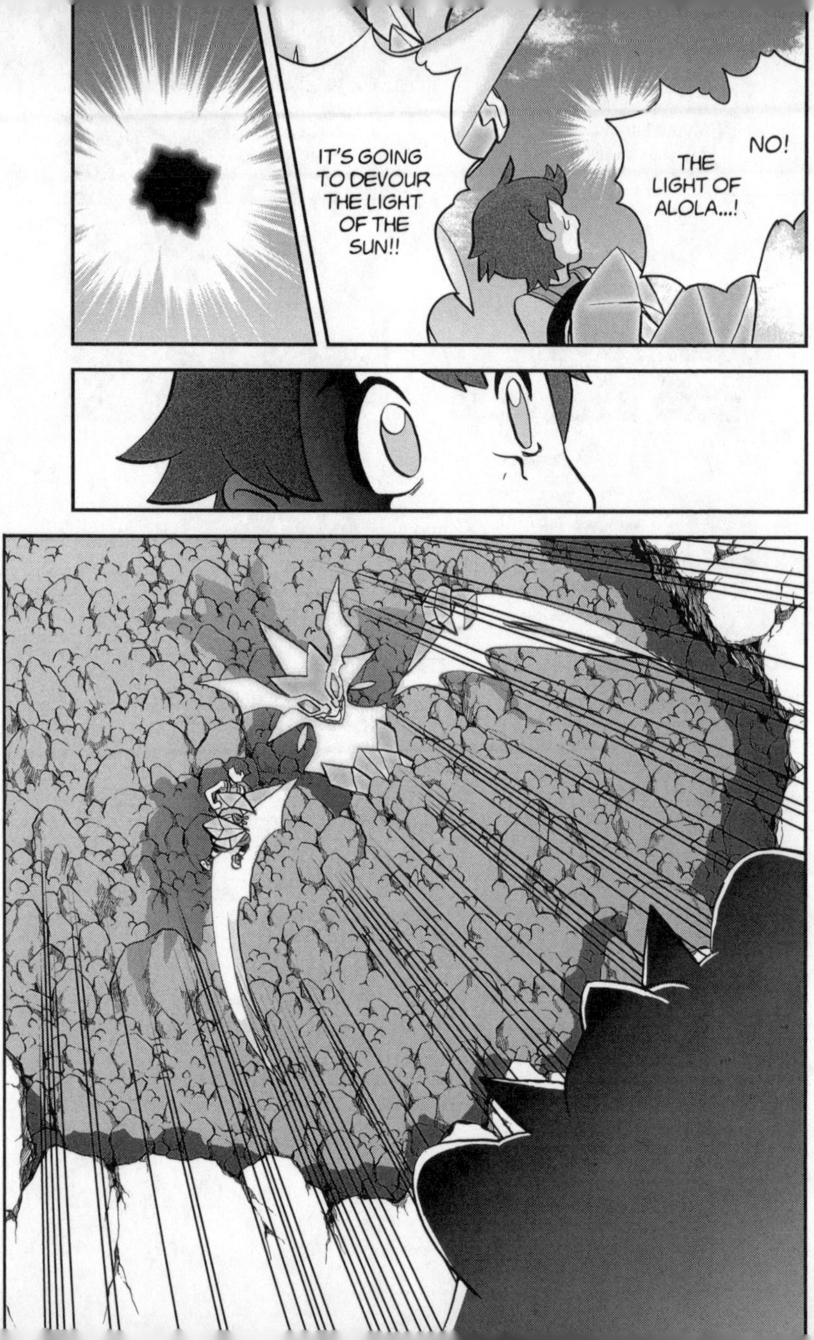
NO!
THE LIGHT OF ALOLA...!
IT'S GOING TO DEVOUR THE LIGHT OF THE SUN!!

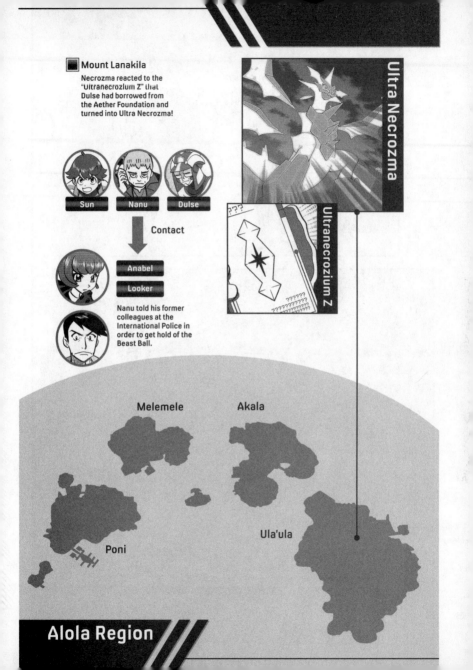

Mount Lanakila

Necrozma reacted to the "Ultranecrozium Z" that Dulse had borrowed from the Aether Foundation and turned into Ultra Necrozma!

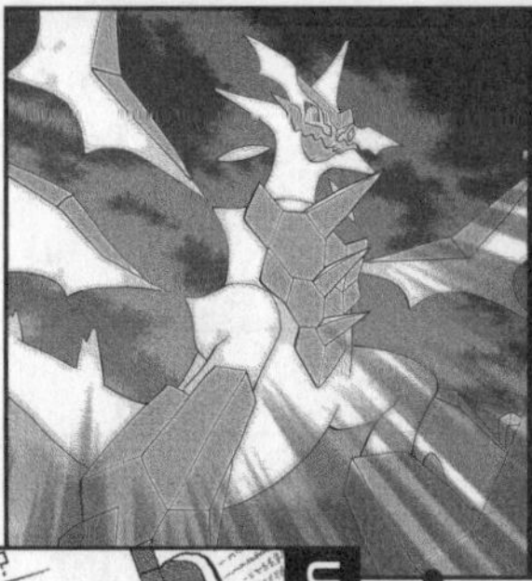

Ultra Necrozma

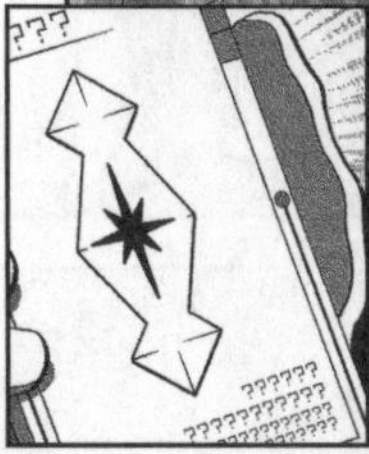
???
??????
???????????

Ultranecrozium Z

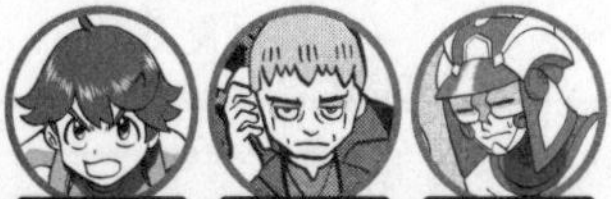

Sun | Nanu | Dulse

Contact

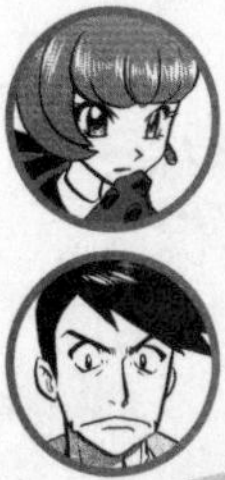

Anabel

Looker

Nanu told his former colleagues at the International Police in order to get hold of the Beast Ball.

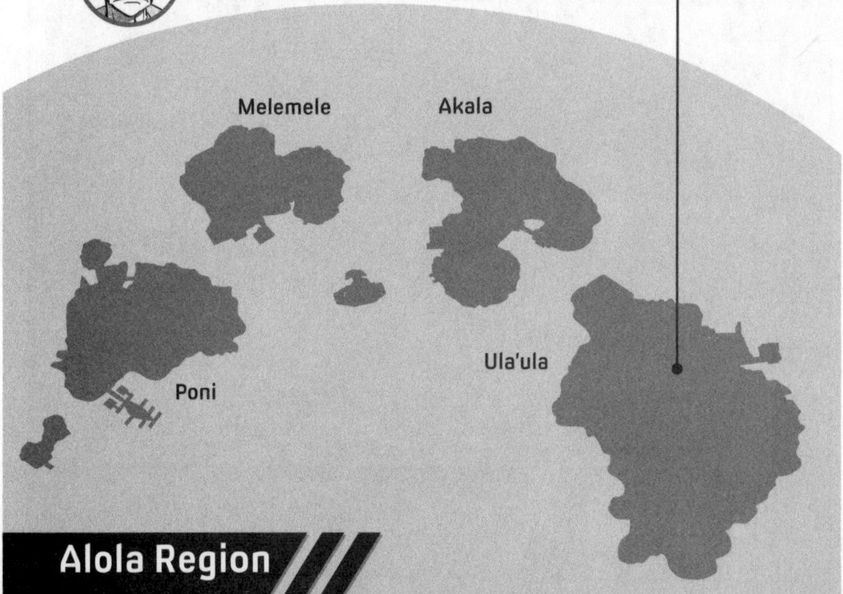
Melemele
Akala
Ula'ula
Poni

Alola Region

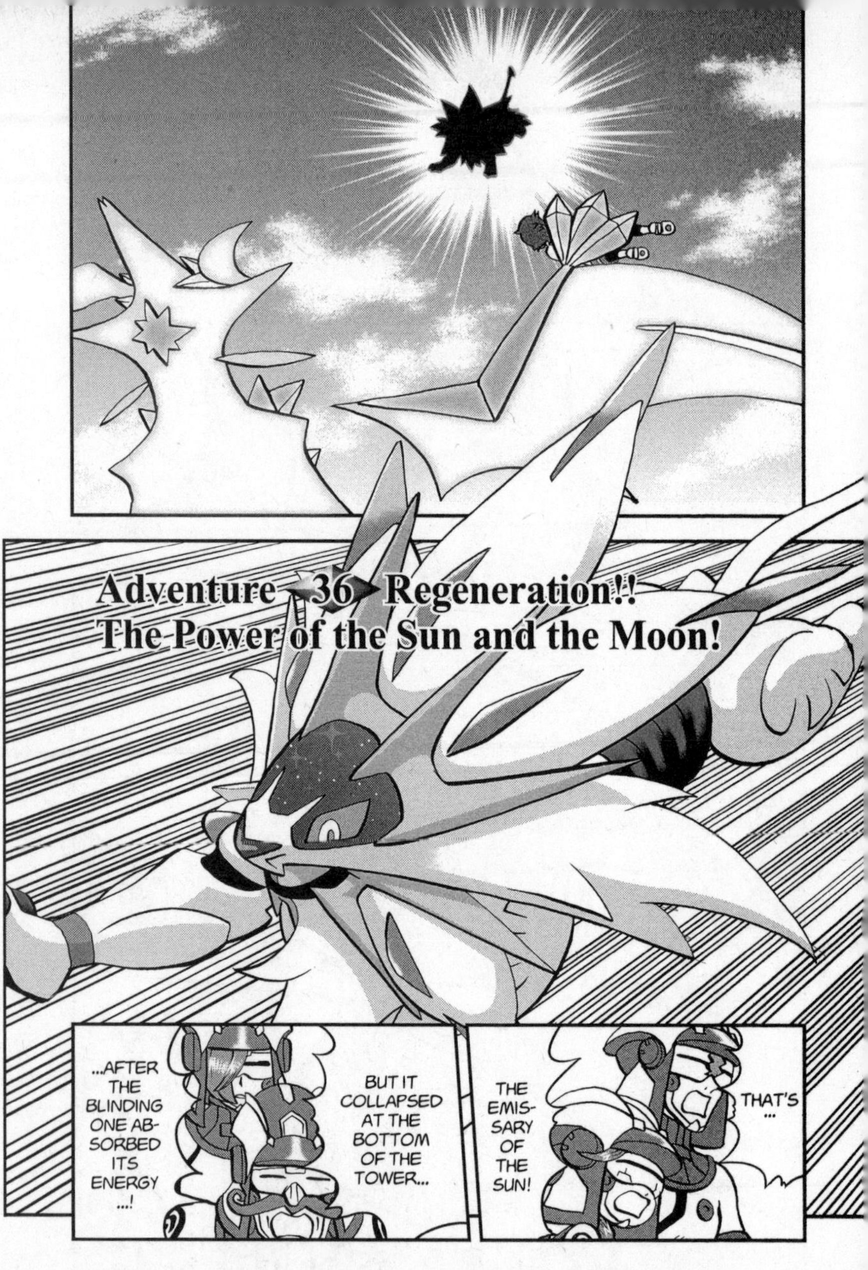
Adventure 36 Regeneration!! The Power of the Sun and the Moon!
THAT'S...
THE EMISSARY OF THE SUN!
BUT IT COLLAPSED AT THE BOTTOM OF THE TOWER...
...AFTER THE BLINDING ONE ABSORBED ITS ENERGY...!

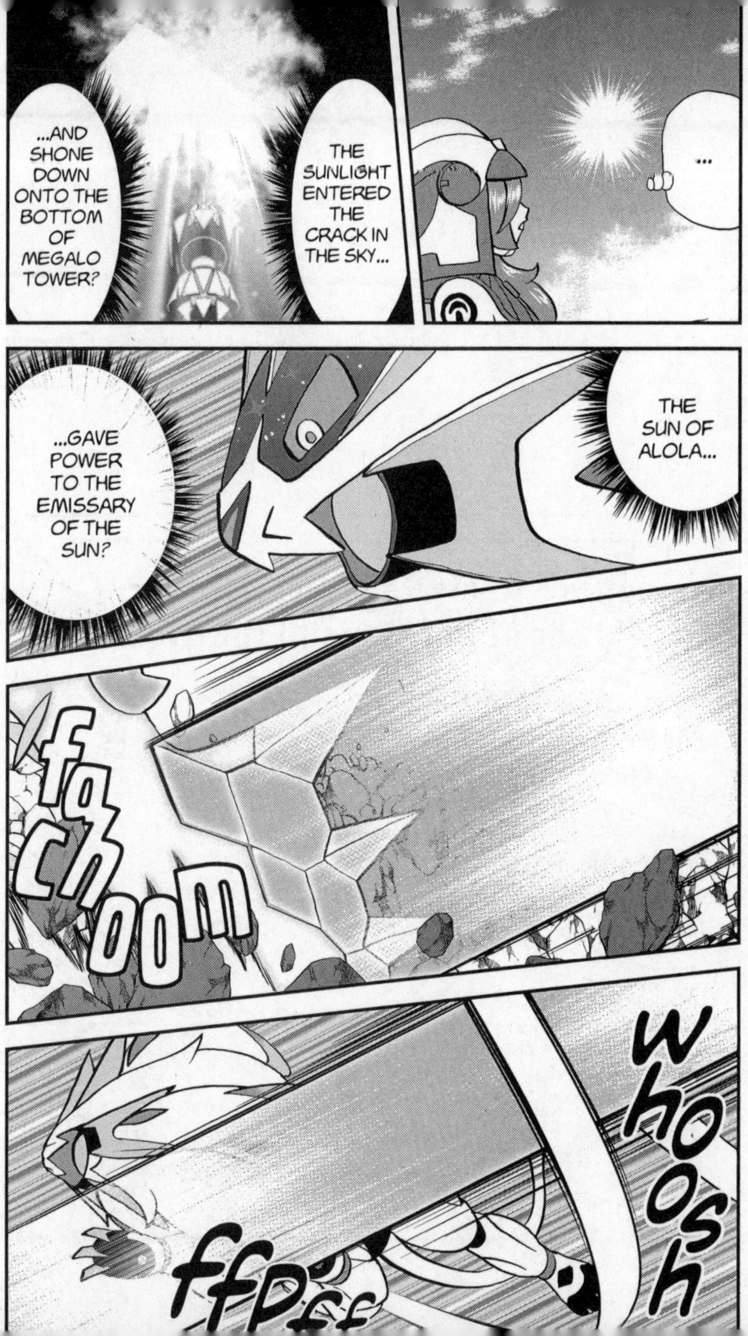
...
THE SUNLIGHT ENTERED THE CRACK IN THE SKY...
...AND SHONE DOWN ONTO THE BOTTOM OF MEGALO TOWER?
THE SUN OF ALOLA...
...GAVE POWER TO THE EMISSARY OF THE SUN?
fachoom
whoosh

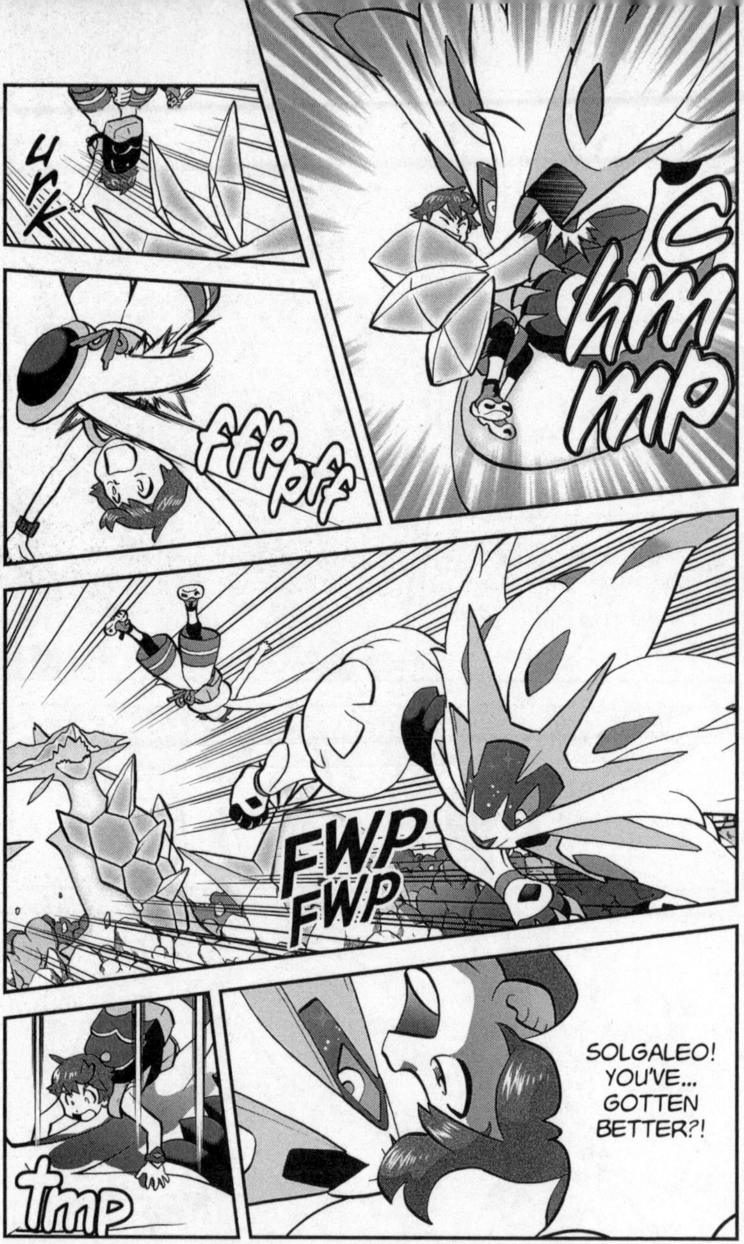
Chmmp
urk
ffppff
FWP FWP
SOLGALEO! YOU'VE... GOTTEN BETTER?!
tmp

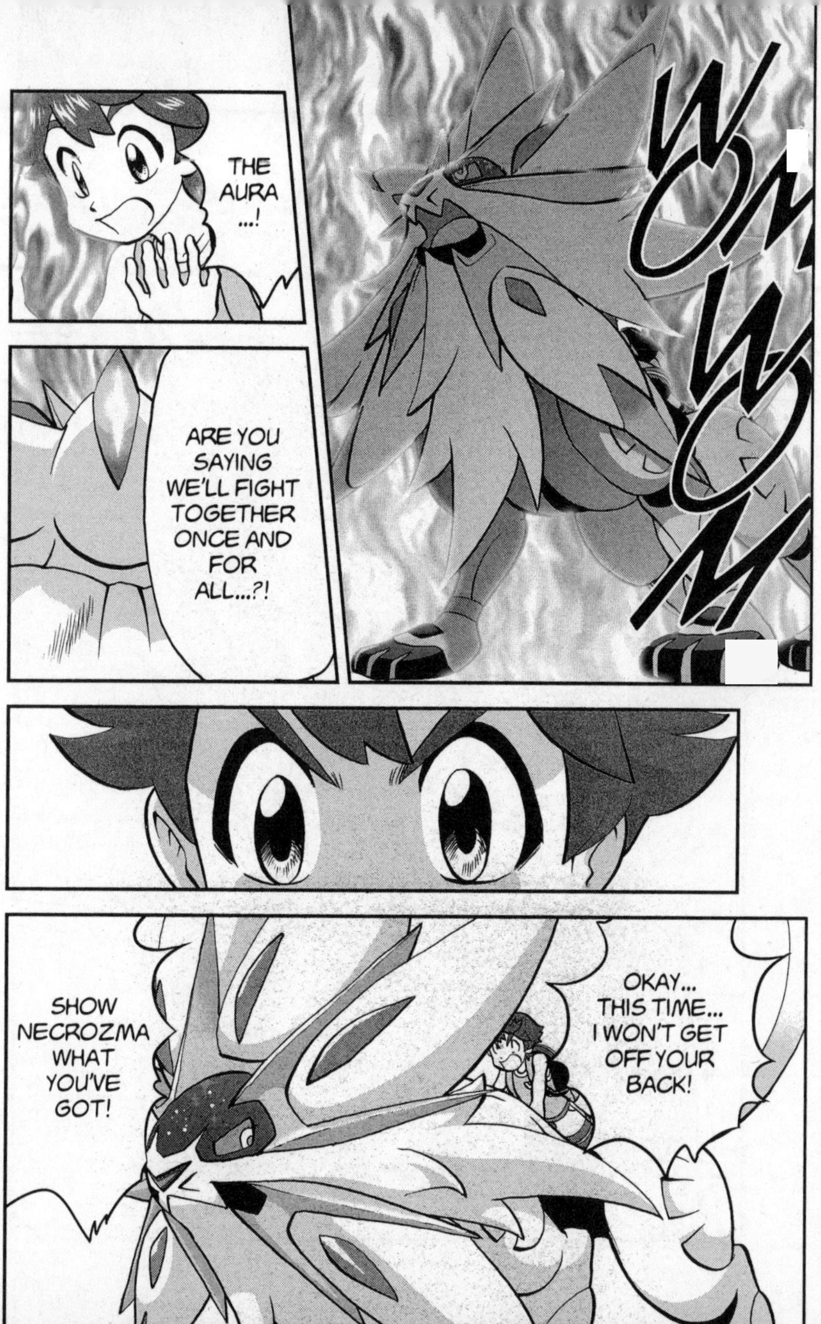
THE AURA ...!
ARE YOU SAYING WE'LL FIGHT TOGETHER ONCE AND FOR ALL...?!
OKAY... THIS TIME... I WON'T GET OFF YOUR BACK!
SHOW NECROZMA WHAT YOU'VE GOT!

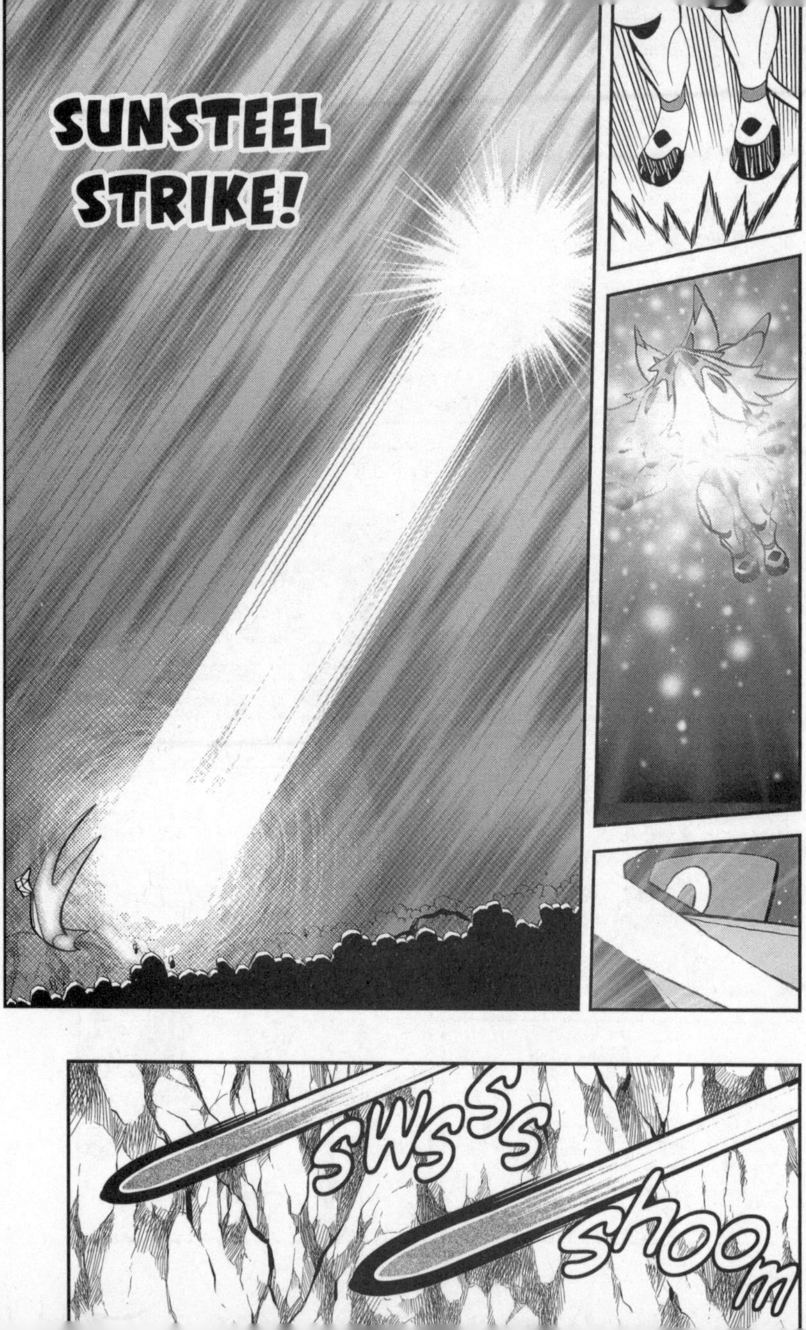
SUNSTEEL STRIKE!
SWSSS
SHOOM

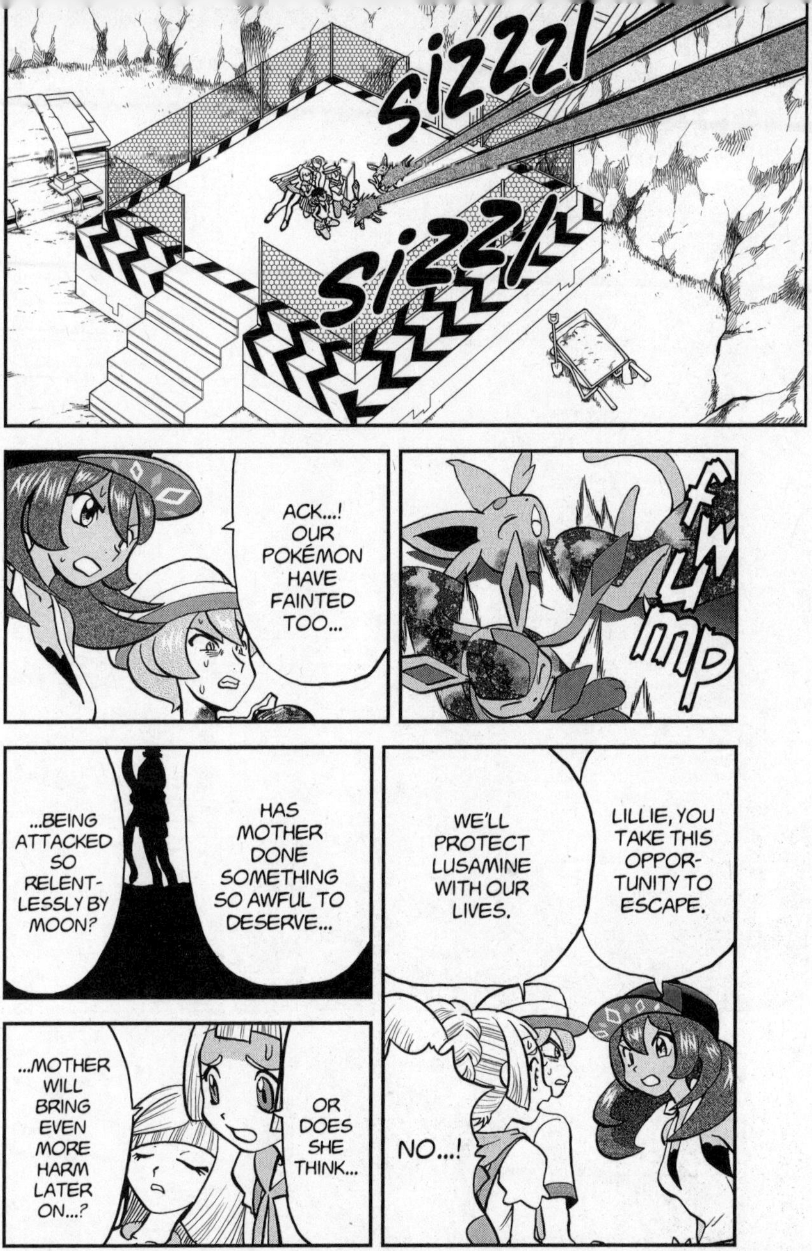
SIZZZ!
SIZZZ
FWUMP
ACK...! OUR POKÉMON HAVE FAINTED TOO...
LILLIE, YOU TAKE THIS OPPOR-TUNITY TO ESCAPE.
WE'LL PROTECT LUSAMINE WITH OUR LIVES.
NO...!
HAS MOTHER DONE SOMETHING SO AWFUL TO DESERVE...
...BEING ATTACKED SO RELENT-LESSLY BY MOON?
OR DOES SHE THINK...
...MOTHER WILL BRING EVEN MORE HARM LATER ON...?

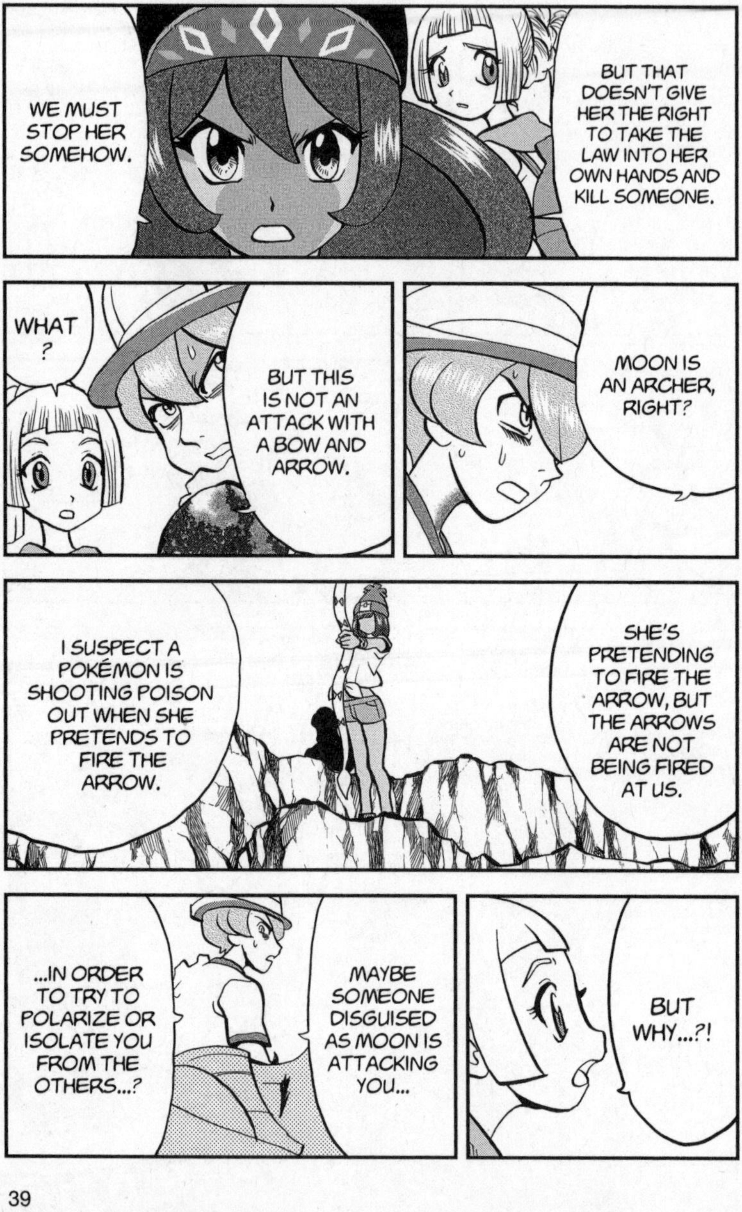
BUT THAT DOESN'T GIVE HER THE RIGHT TO TAKE THE LAW INTO HER OWN HANDS AND KILL SOMEONE.
WE MUST STOP HER SOMEHOW.
MOON IS AN ARCHER, RIGHT?
BUT THIS IS NOT AN ATTACK WITH A BOW AND ARROW.
WHAT?
SHE'S PRETENDING TO FIRE THE ARROW, BUT THE ARROWS ARE NOT BEING FIRED AT US.
I SUSPECT A POKÉMON IS SHOOTING POISON OUT WHEN SHE PRETENDS TO FIRE THE ARROW.
BUT WHY...?!
MAYBE SOMEONE DISGUISED AS MOON IS ATTACKING YOU...
...IN ORDER TO TRY TO POLARIZE OR ISOLATE YOU FROM THE OTHERS...?

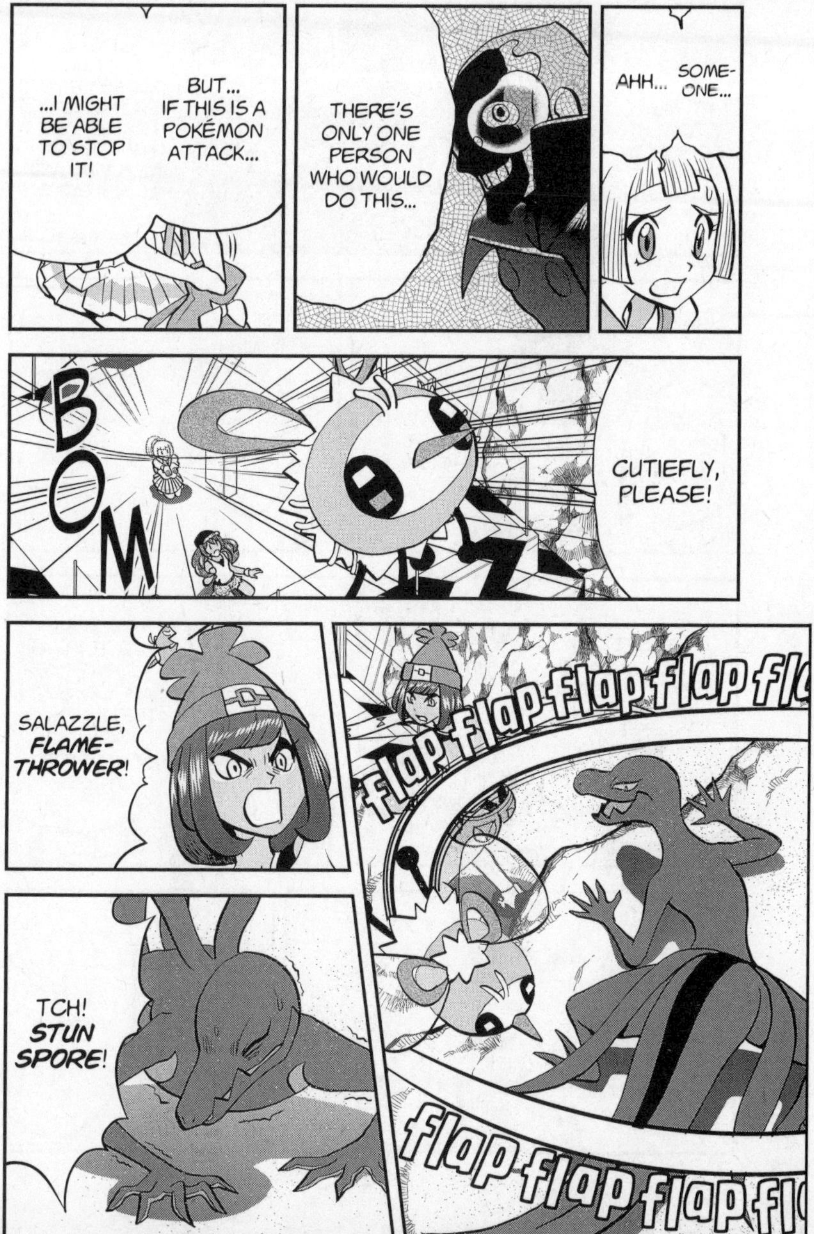
AHH... SOME-ONE...
THERE'S ONLY ONE PERSON WHO WOULD DO THIS...
BUT... IF THIS IS A POKÉMON ATTACK...
...I MIGHT BE ABLE TO STOP IT!
CUTIEFLY, PLEASE!
BOM
flap flap flap flap fl
flap flap flap fl
SALAZZLE, FLAME-THROWER!
TCH! STUN SPORE!

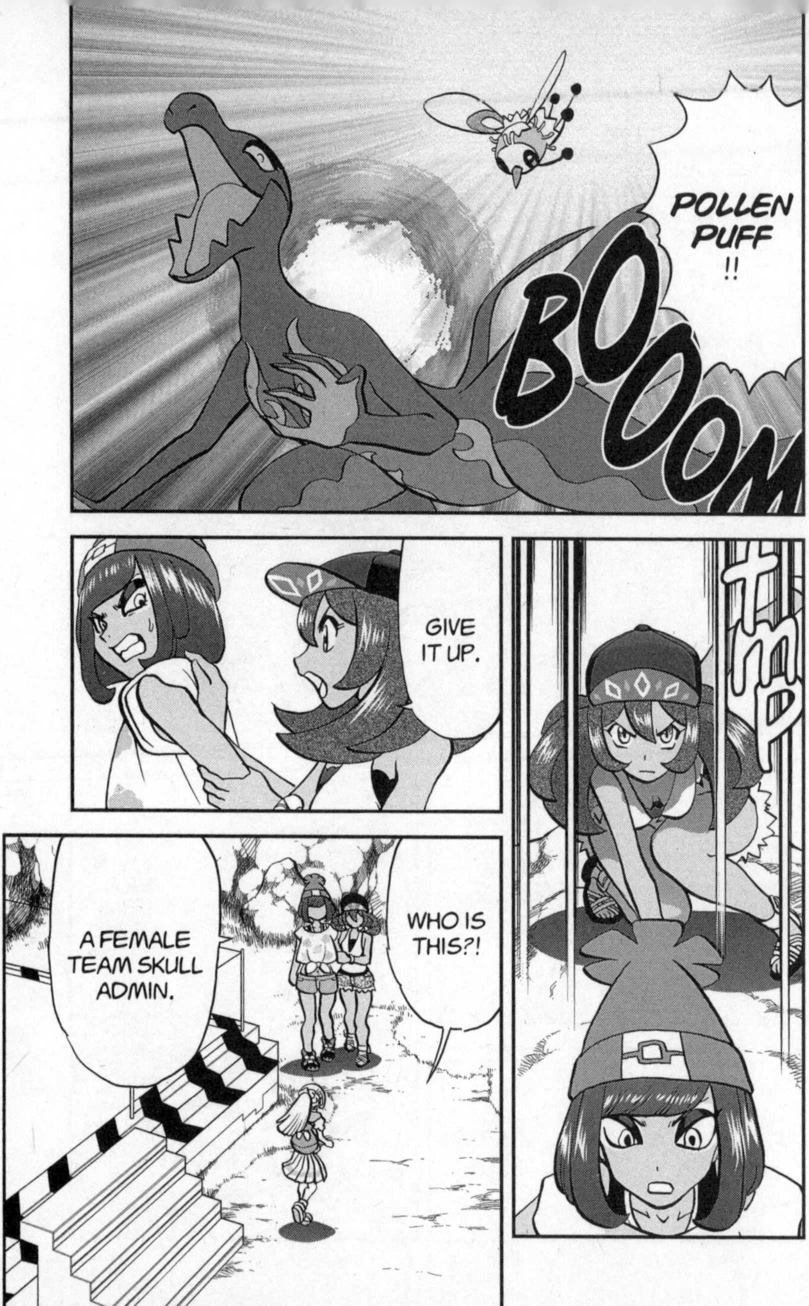
POLLEN PUFF !!
BOOOOM
TMP
GIVE IT UP.
WHO IS THIS?!
A FEMALE TEAM SKULL ADMIN.

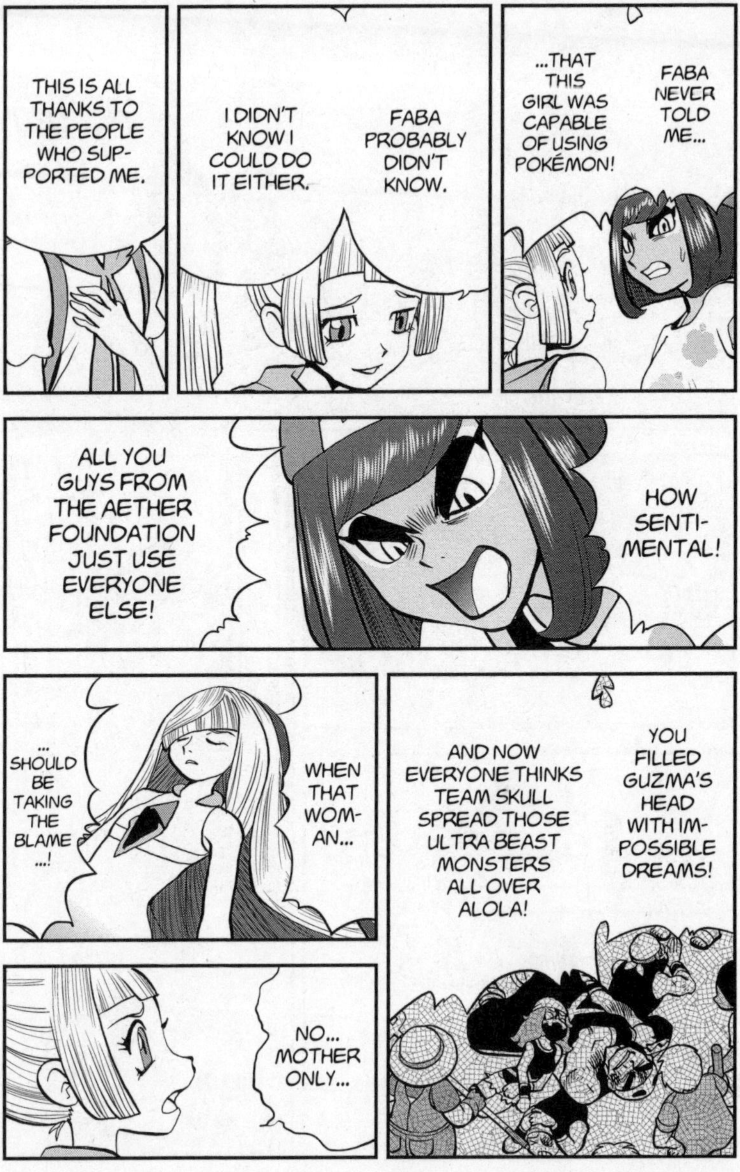
FABA NEVER TOLD ME...
...THAT THIS GIRL WAS CAPABLE OF USING POKÉMON!
FABA PROBABLY DIDN'T KNOW.
I DIDN'T KNOW I COULD DO IT EITHER.
THIS IS ALL THANKS TO THE PEOPLE WHO SUP-PORTED ME.
HOW SENTI-MENTAL!
ALL YOU GUYS FROM THE AETHER FOUNDATION JUST USE EVERYONE ELSE!
YOU FILLED GUZMA'S HEAD WITH IM-POSSIBLE DREAMS!
AND NOW EVERYONE THINKS TEAM SKULL SPREAD THOSE ULTRA BEAST MONSTERS ALL OVER ALOLA!
WHEN THAT WOM-AN...
...SHOULD BE TAKING THE BLAME...!
NO... MOTHER ONLY...

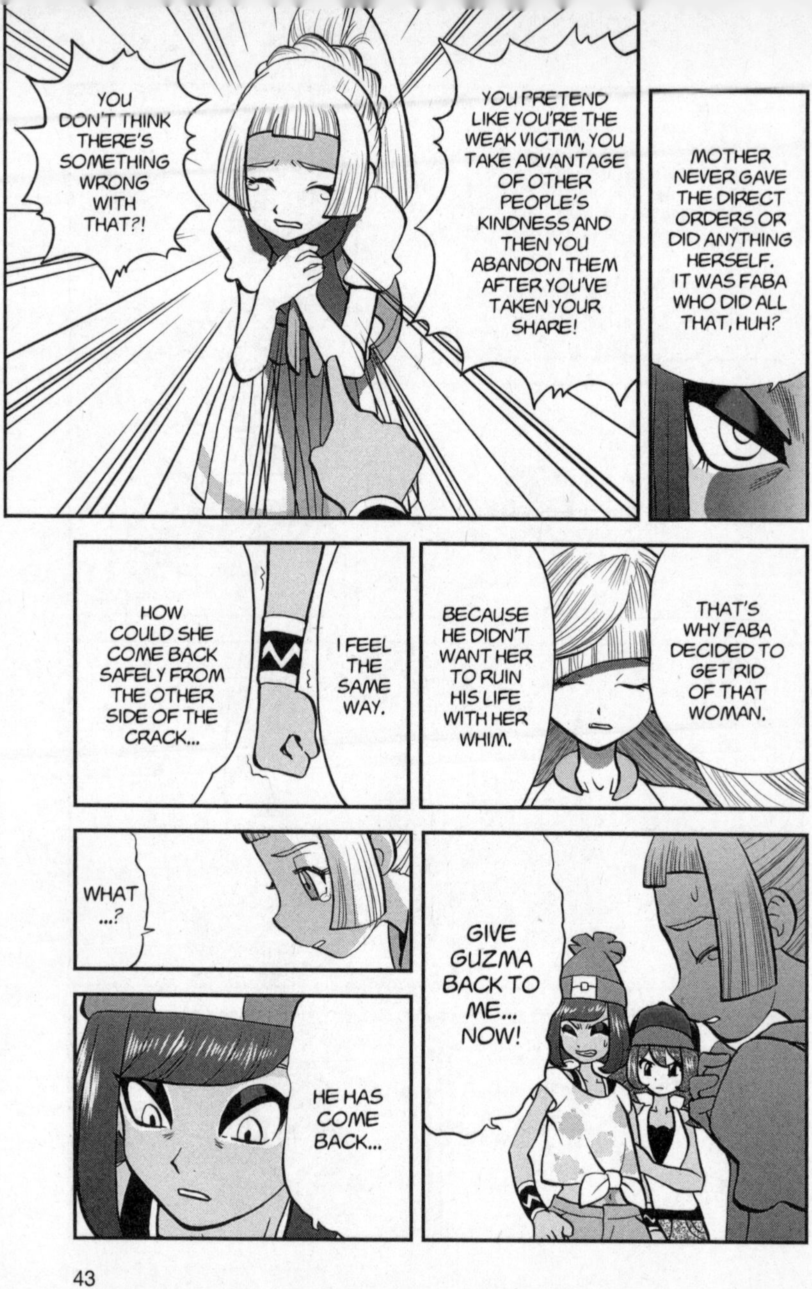
MOTHER NEVER GAVE THE DIRECT ORDERS OR DID ANYTHING HERSELF. IT WAS FABA WHO DID ALL THAT, HUH?
YOU PRETEND LIKE YOU'RE THE WEAK VICTIM, YOU TAKE ADVANTAGE OF OTHER PEOPLE'S KINDNESS AND THEN YOU ABANDON THEM AFTER YOU'VE TAKEN YOUR SHARE!
YOU DON'T THINK THERE'S SOMETHING WRONG WITH THAT?!
THAT'S WHY FABA DECIDED TO GET RID OF THAT WOMAN.
BECAUSE HE DIDN'T WANT HER TO RUIN HIS LIFE WITH HER WHIM.
I FEEL THE SAME WAY.
HOW COULD SHE COME BACK SAFELY FROM THE OTHER SIDE OF THE CRACK...
GIVE GUZMA BACK TO ME... NOW!
WHAT ...?
HE HAS COME BACK...

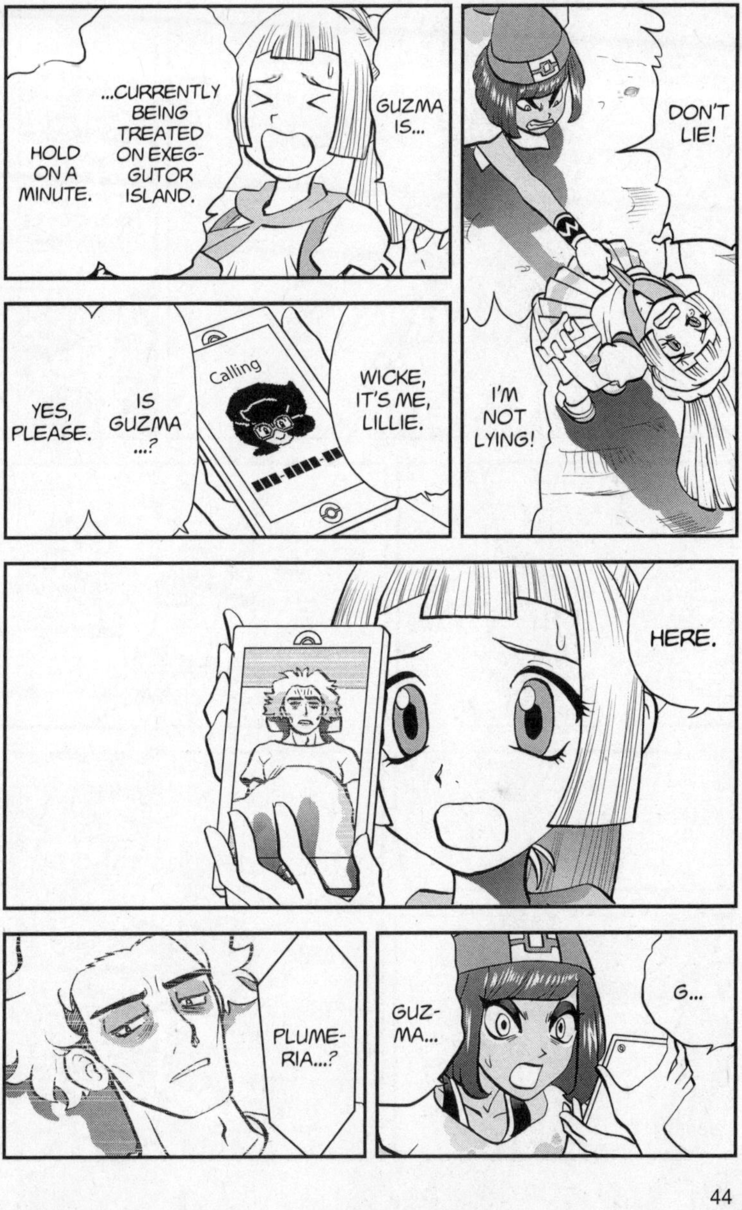
DON'T LIE!
I'M NOT LYING!
GUZMA IS...
...CURRENTLY BEING TREATED ON EXEGGUTOR ISLAND.
HOLD ON A MINUTE.
WICKE, IT'S ME, LILLIE.
Calling
IS GUZMA...?
YES, PLEASE.
HERE.
G...
GUZMA...
PLUMERIA...?

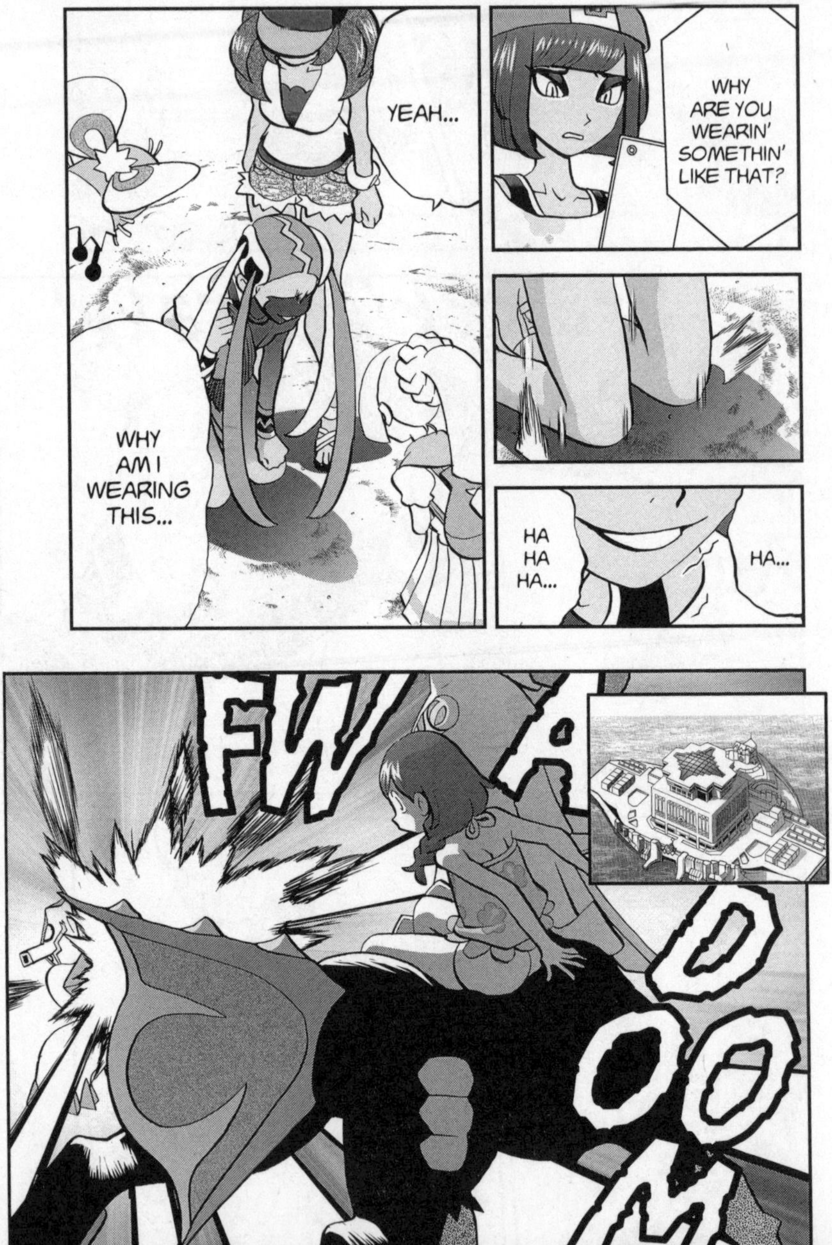
WHY ARE YOU WEARIN' SOMETHIN' LIKE THAT?
HA...
HA HA HA...
YEAH...
WHY AM I WEARING THIS...
FWOOOM

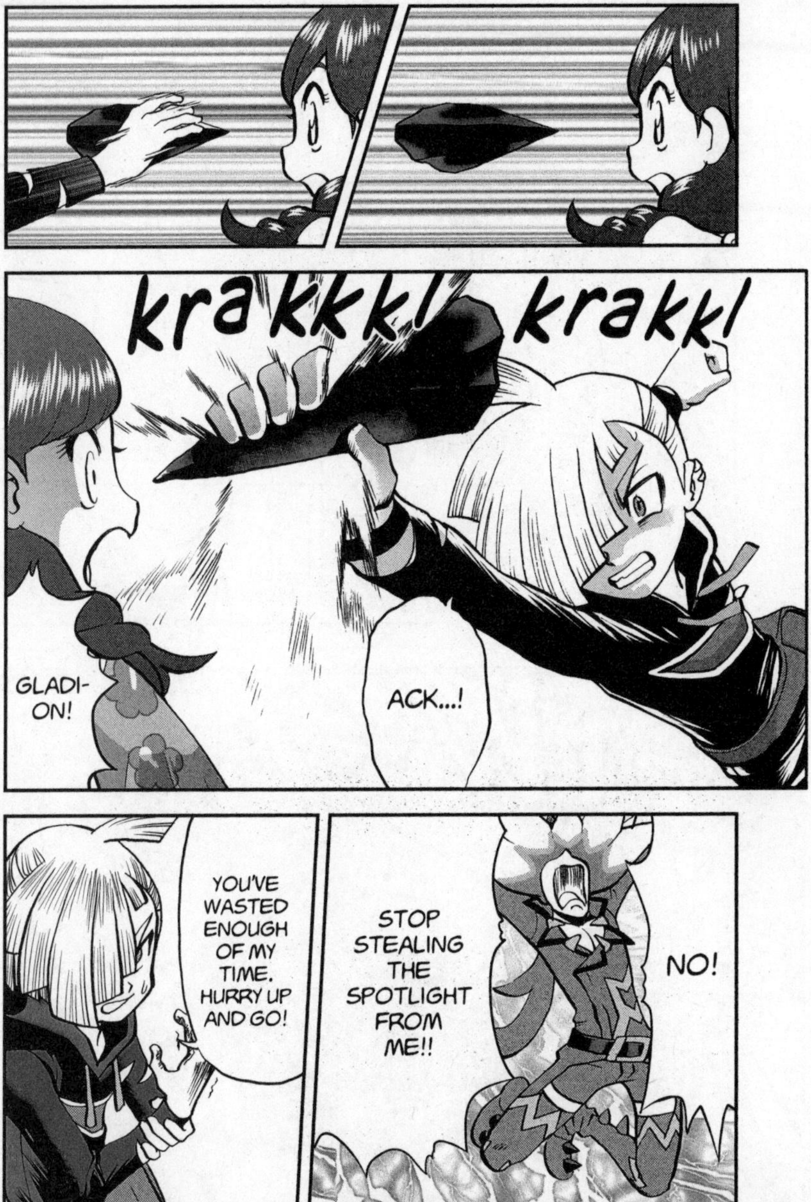
krakk!
krakkk!
ACK...!
GLADI-ON!
NO!
STOP STEALING THE SPOTLIGHT FROM ME!!
YOU'VE WASTED ENOUGH OF MY TIME. HURRY UP AND GO!

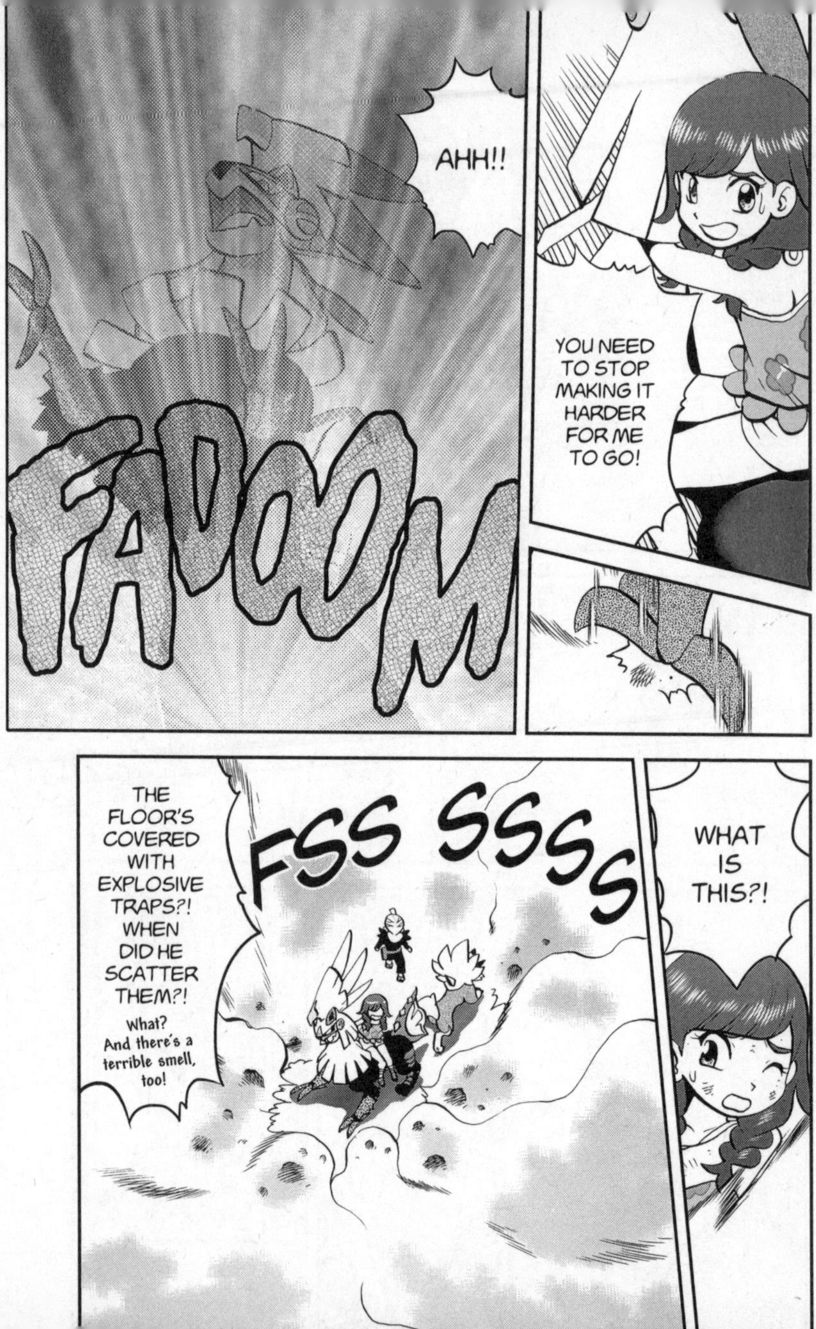
YOU NEED TO STOP MAKING IT HARDER FOR ME TO GO!
AHH!!
FADOOM
WHAT IS THIS?!
FSS SSSSS
THE FLOOR'S COVERED WITH EXPLOSIVE TRAPS?! WHEN DID HE SCATTER THEM?!
What? And there's a terrible smell, too!

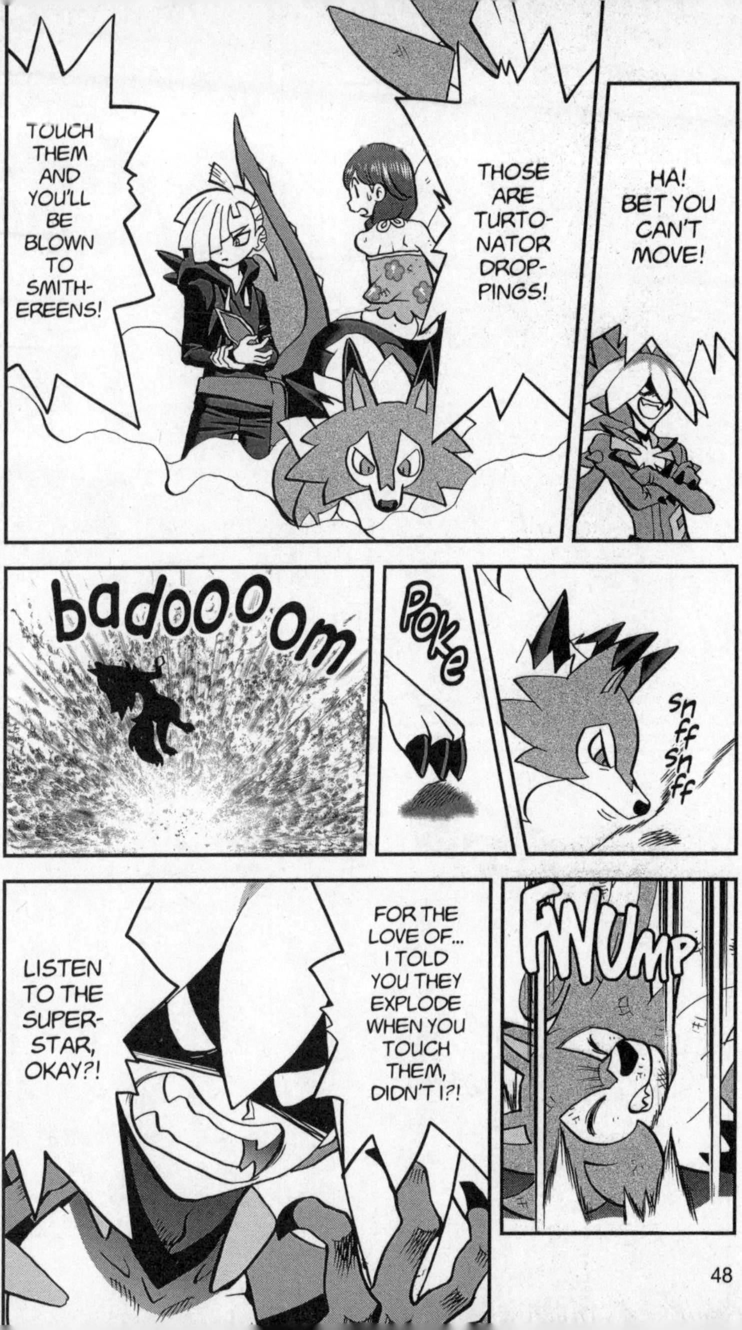
HA! BET YOU CAN'T MOVE!
THOSE ARE TURTO-NATOR DROP-PINGS!
TOUCH THEM AND YOU'LL BE BLOWN TO SMITH-EREENS!
snff snff
POKE
badooooom
FWUMP
FOR THE LOVE OF... I TOLD YOU THEY EXPLODE WHEN YOU TOUCH THEM, DIDN'T I?!
LISTEN TO THE SUPER-STAR, OKAY?!

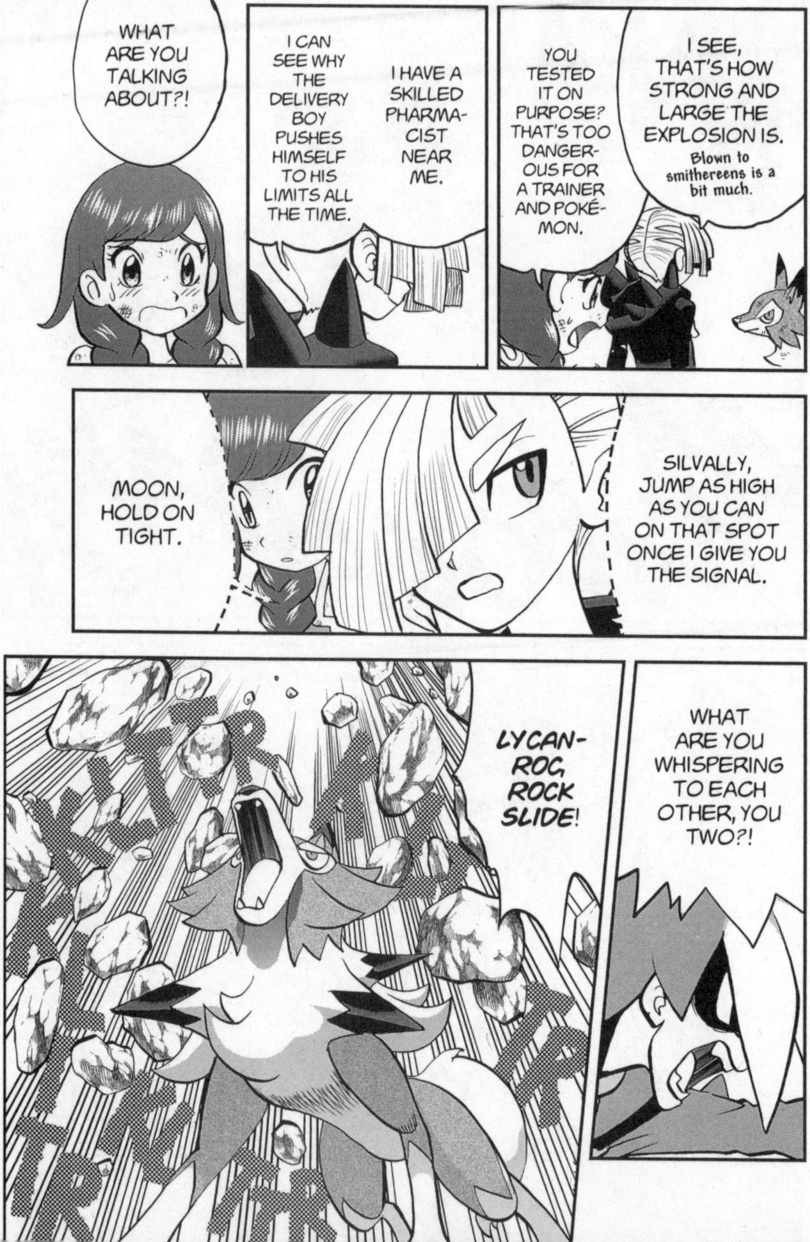
I SEE, THAT'S HOW STRONG AND LARGE THE EXPLOSION IS.
Blown to smithereens is a bit much.
YOU TESTED IT ON PURPOSE? THAT'S TOO DANGEROUS FOR A TRAINER AND POKÉMON.
I HAVE A SKILLED PHARMACIST NEAR ME.
I CAN SEE WHY THE DELIVERY BOY PUSHES HIMSELF TO HIS LIMITS ALL THE TIME.
WHAT ARE YOU TALKING ABOUT?!
SILVALLY, JUMP AS HIGH AS YOU CAN ON THAT SPOT ONCE I GIVE YOU THE SIGNAL.
MOON, HOLD ON TIGHT.
WHAT ARE YOU WHISPERING TO EACH OTHER, YOU TWO?!
LYCANROC, ROCK SLIDE!

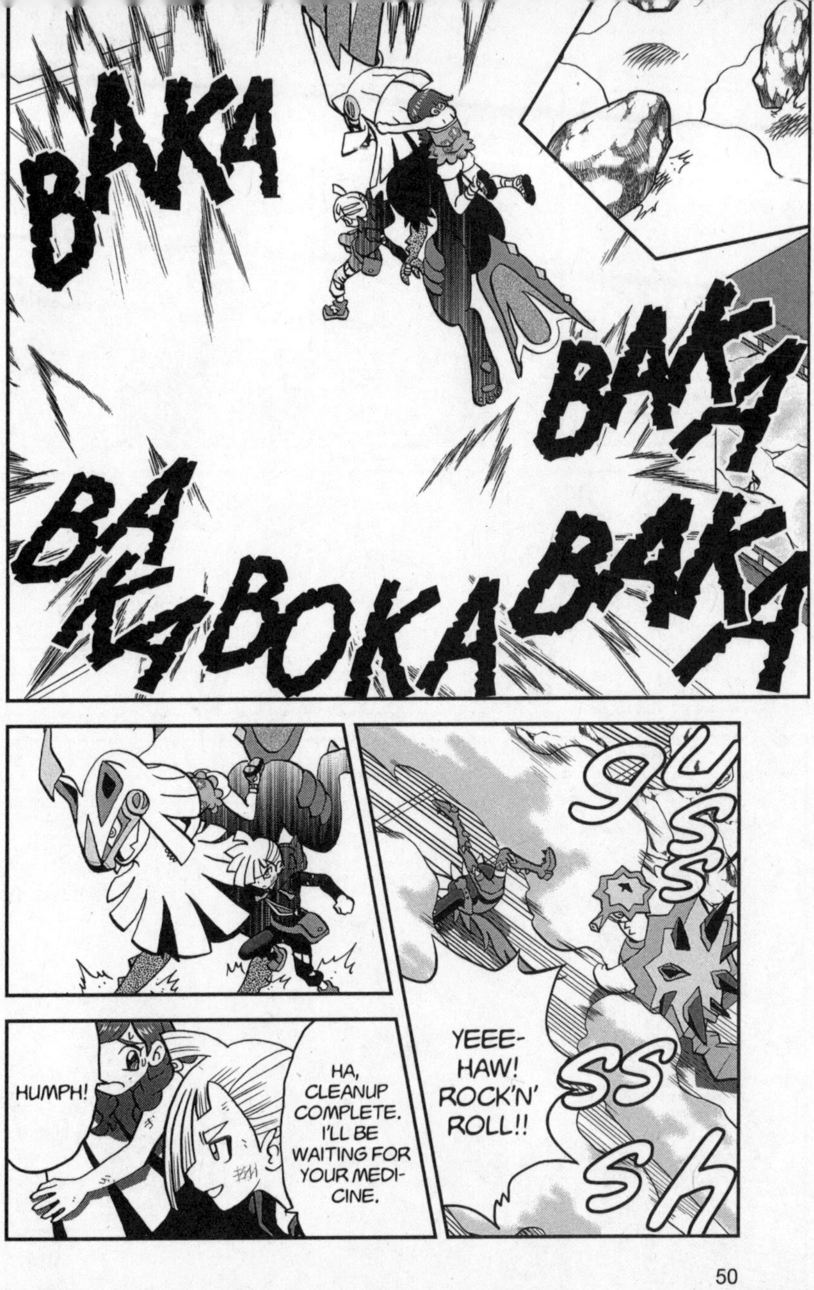
BAKA
BAKA
BAKA
BOKA
BAKA
BAKA
GUSSSSSSH
YEEE-HAW! ROCK'N' ROLL!!
HA, CLEANUP COMPLETE. I'LL BE WAITING FOR YOUR MEDICINE.
HUMPH!

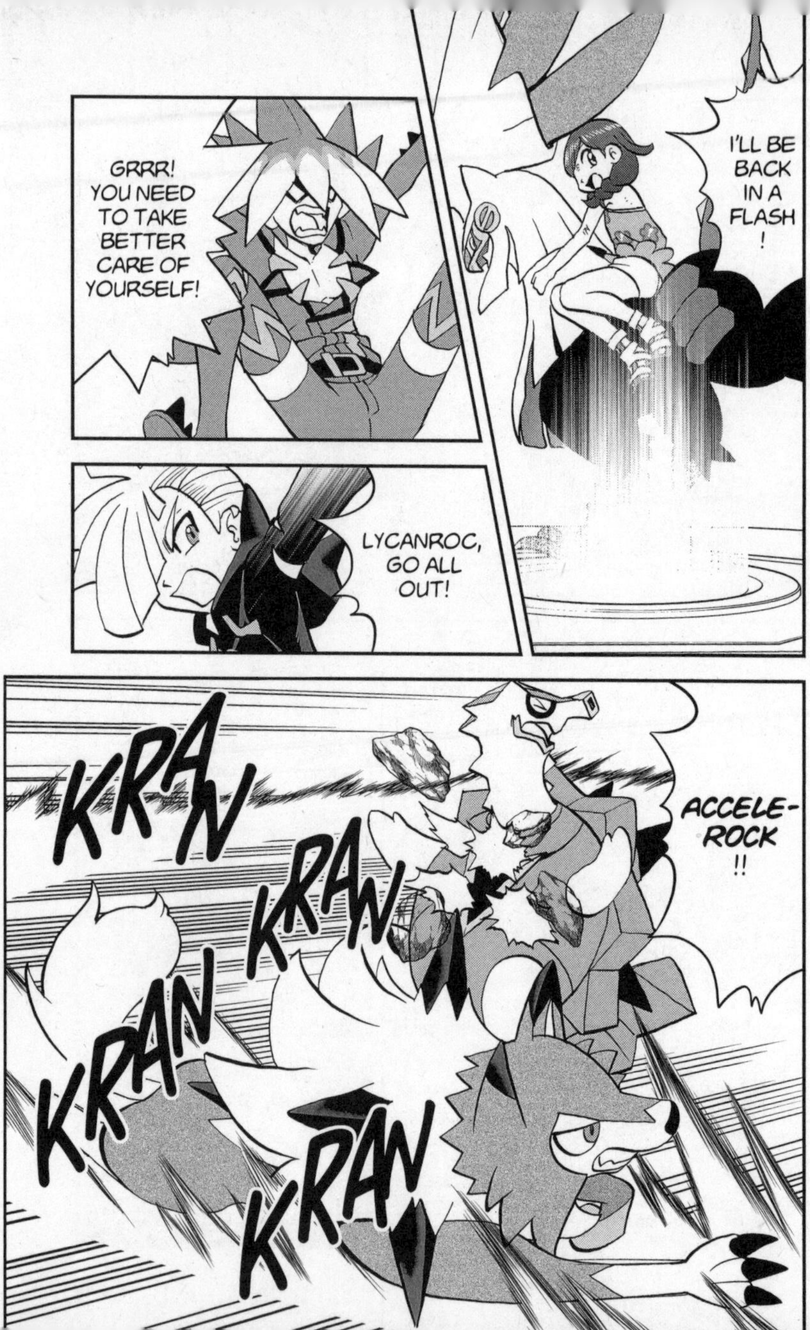
I'LL BE BACK IN A FLASH!
GRRR! YOU NEED TO TAKE BETTER CARE OF YOURSELF!
LYCANROC, GO ALL OUT!
ACCELE-ROCK!!
KRAN
KRAN
KRAN
KRAN

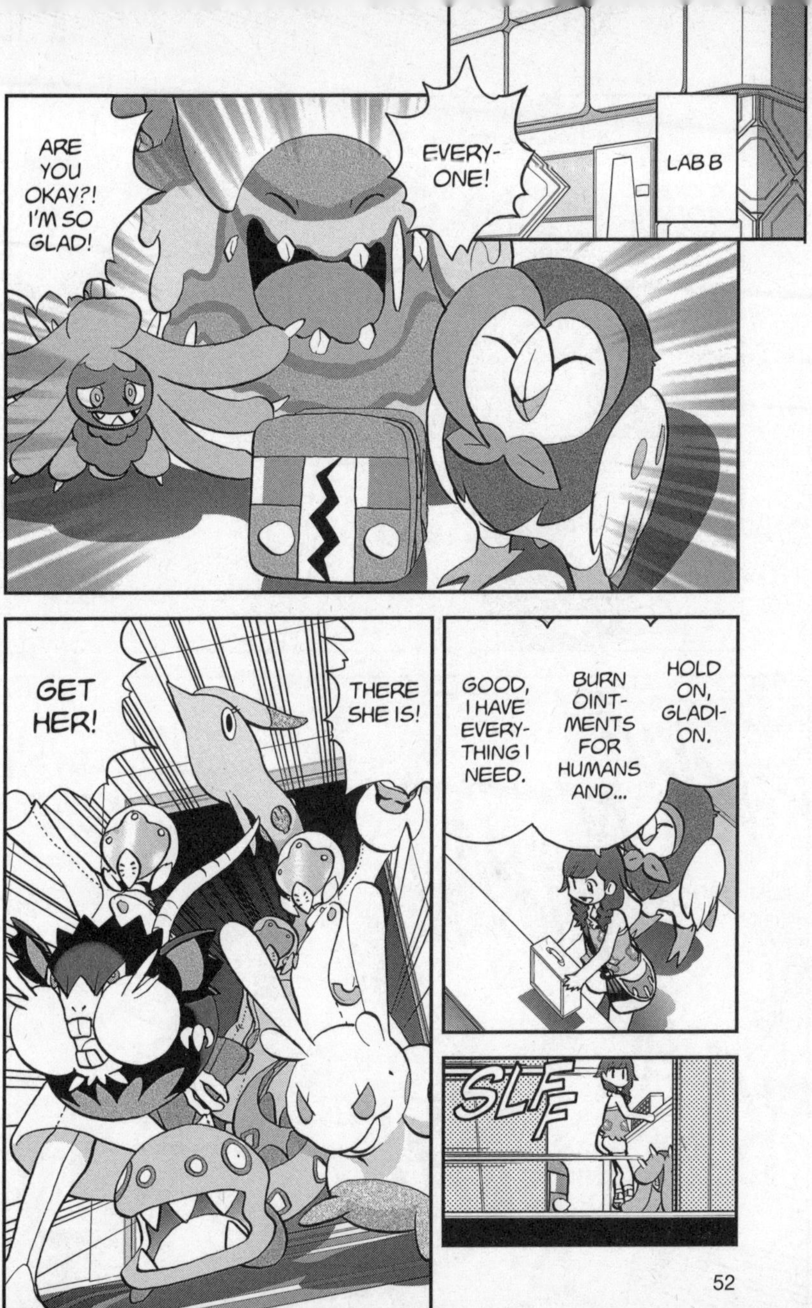
LAB B
EVERY-ONE!
ARE YOU OKAY?! I'M SO GLAD!
HOLD ON, GLADI-ON.
BURN OINT-MENTS FOR HUMANS AND...
GOOD, I HAVE EVERY-THING I NEED.
SLFF
THERE SHE IS!
GET HER!

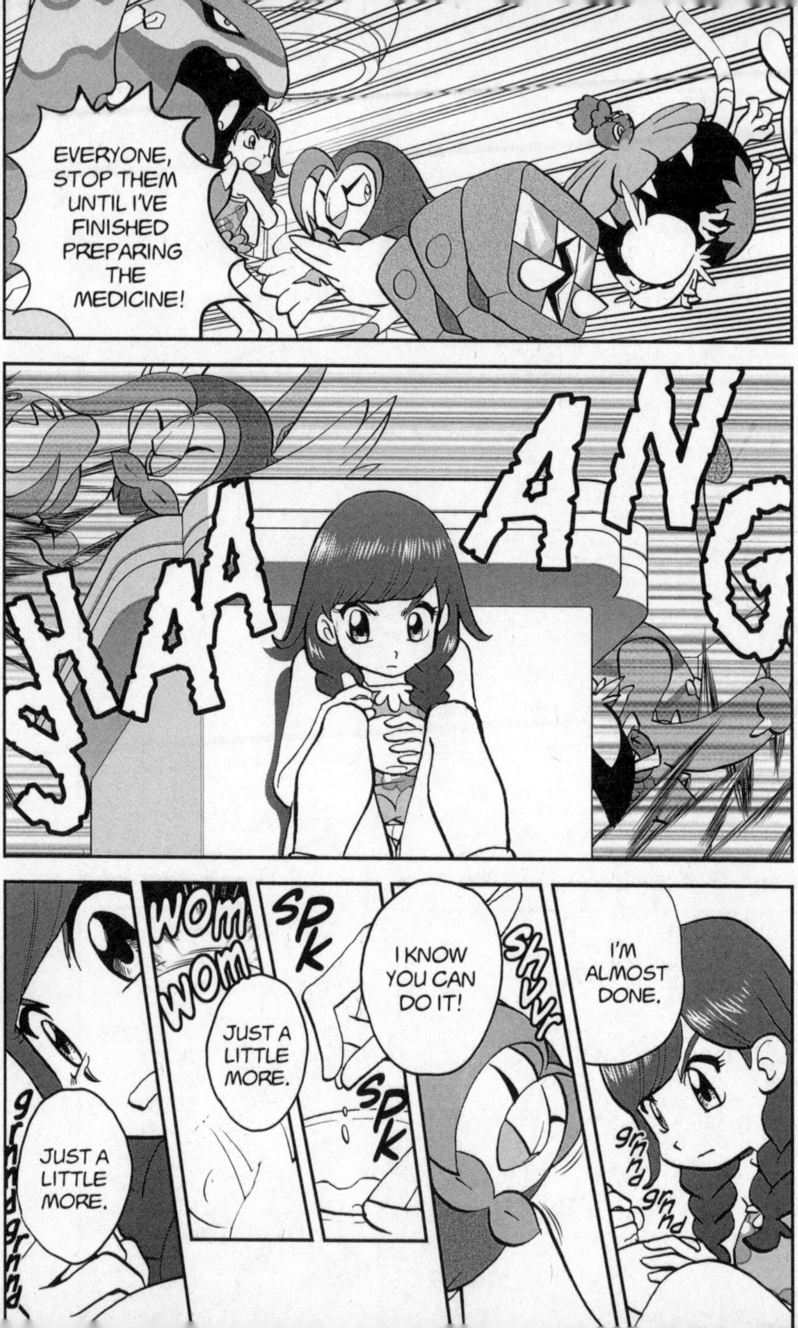
EVERYONE, STOP THEM UNTIL I'VE FINISHED PREPARING THE MEDICINE!
SHAAANG
I'M ALMOST DONE.
I KNOW YOU CAN DO IT!
SPK
JUST A LITTLE MORE.
SPK
WOM WOM
JUST A LITTLE MORE.

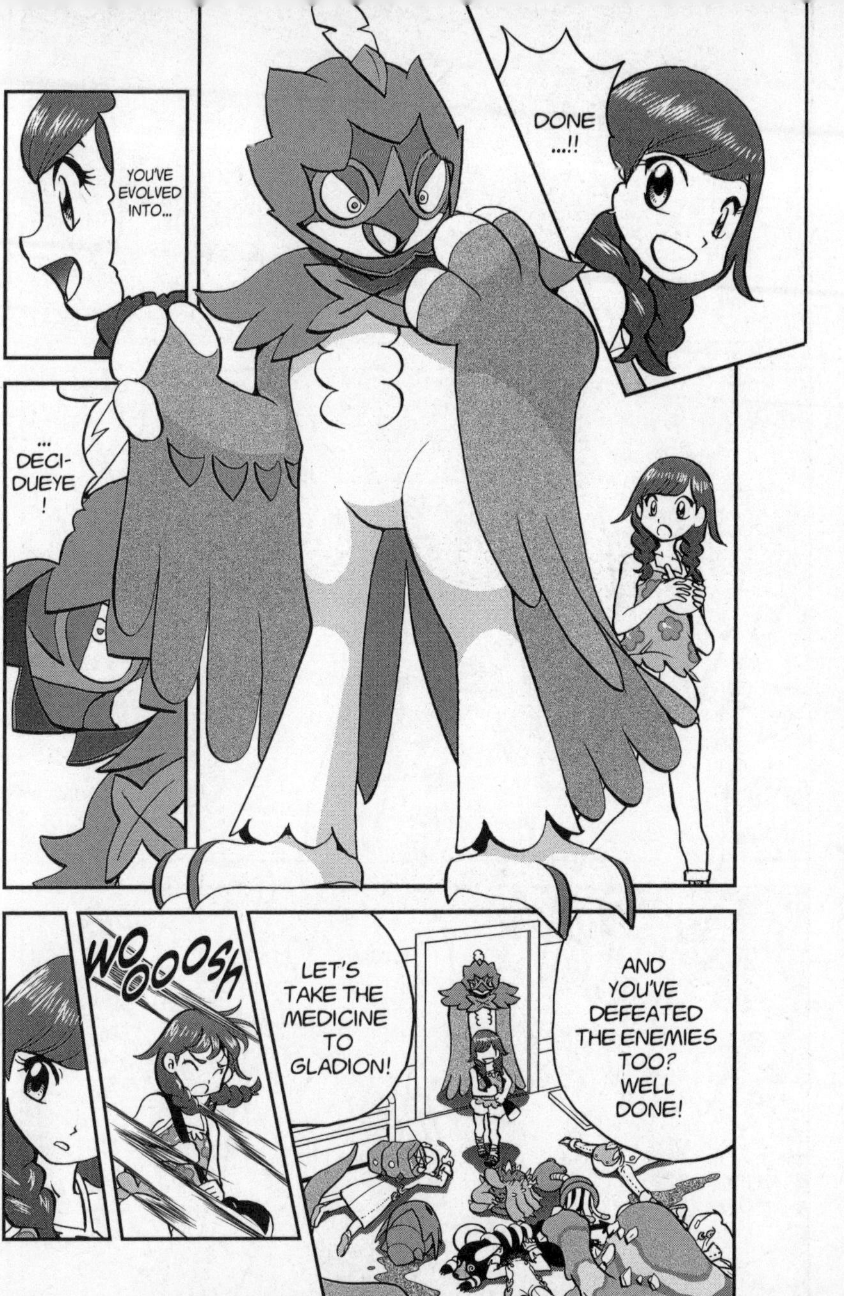
DONE ...!!
YOU'VE EVOLVED INTO...
... DECI-DUEYE !
AND YOU'VE DEFEATED THE ENEMIES TOO? WELL DONE!
LET'S TAKE THE MEDICINE TO GLADION!
WOOOOSH

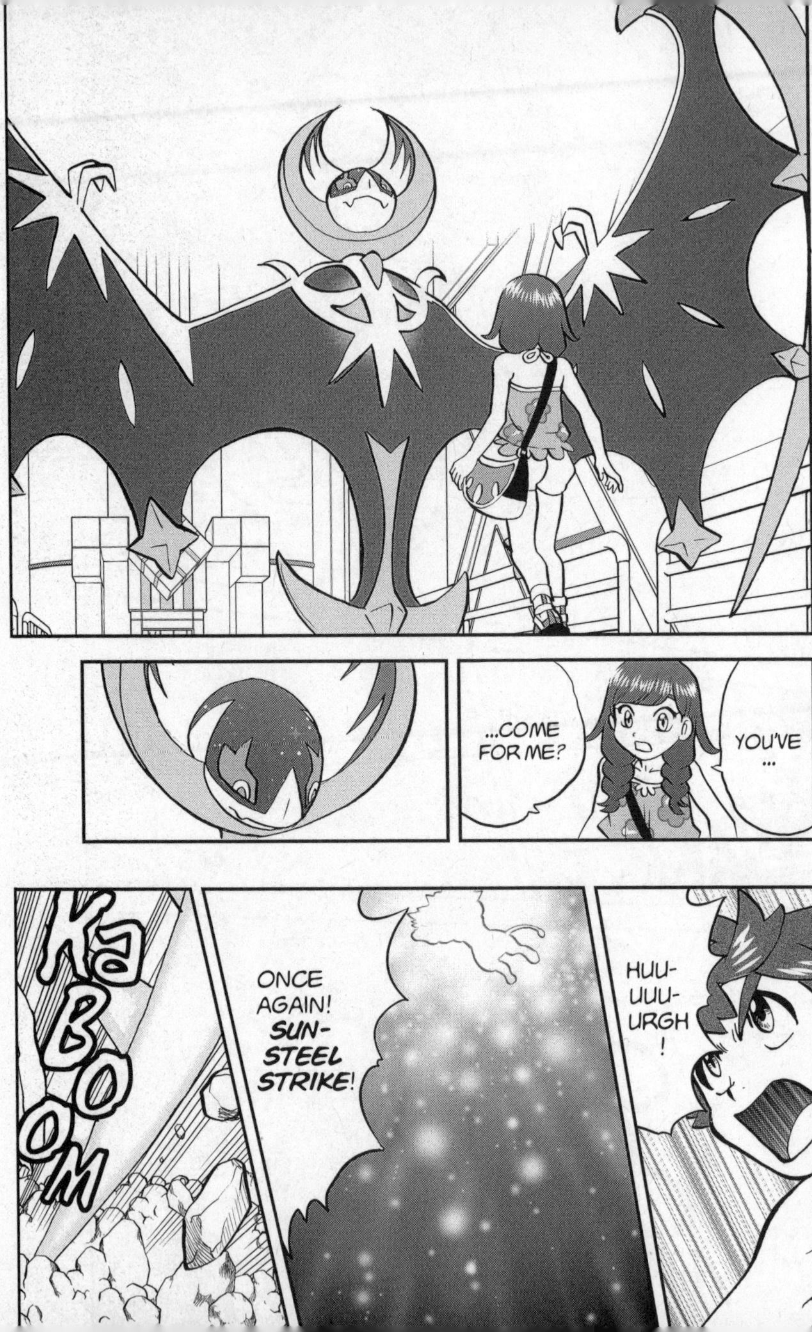
YOU'VE ...
...COME FOR ME?
HUU-UUU-URGH!
ONCE AGAIN! SUN-STEEL STRIKE!
KaBOOM

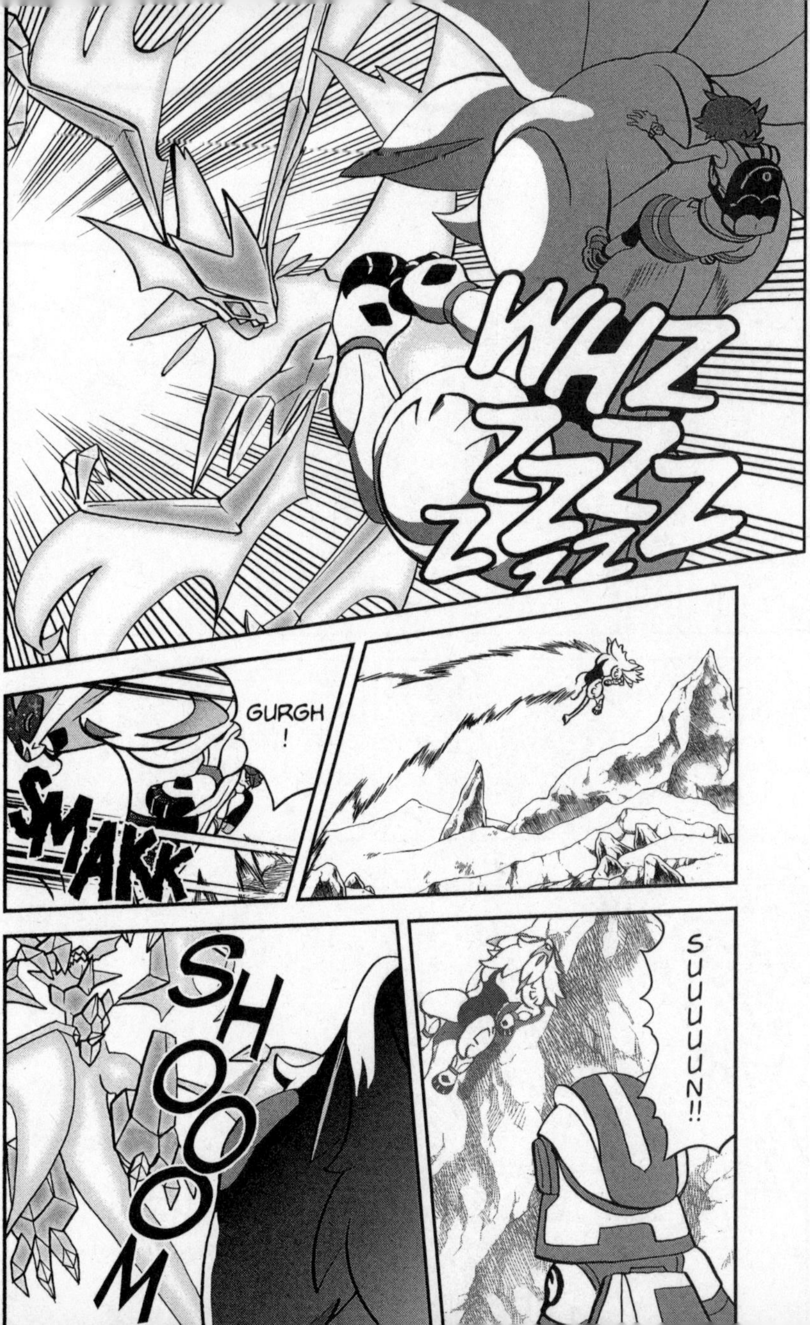
WHIZ ZZZZZ
GURGH!
SMAKK
SUUUUUN!!
SHOOOOM

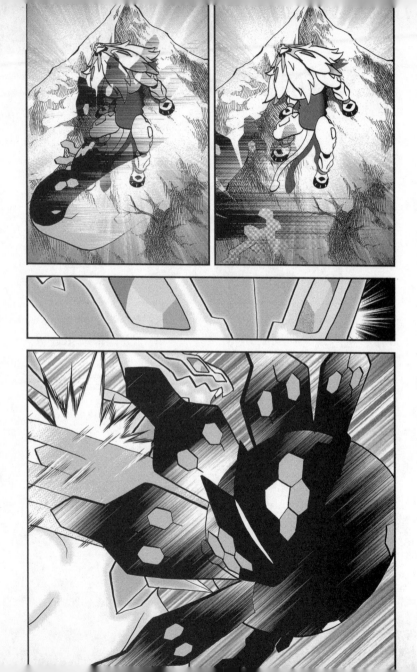

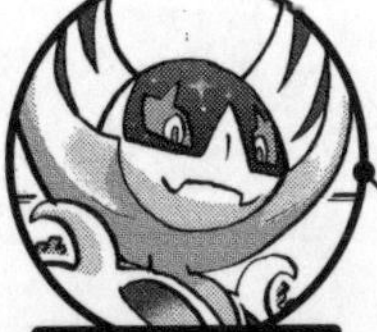

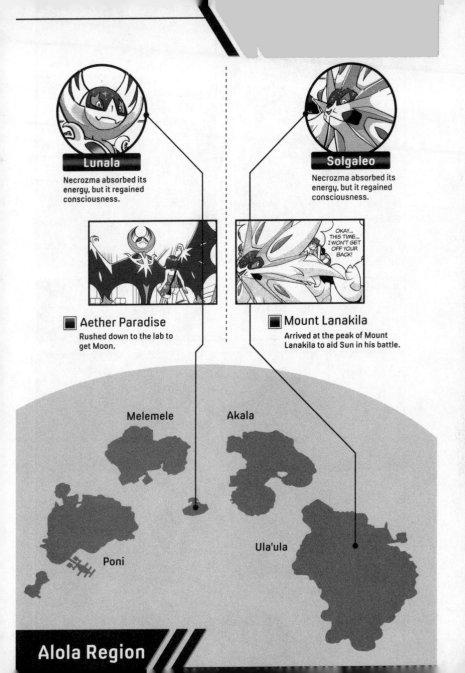

Lunala

Necrozma absorbed its energy, but it regained consciousness.

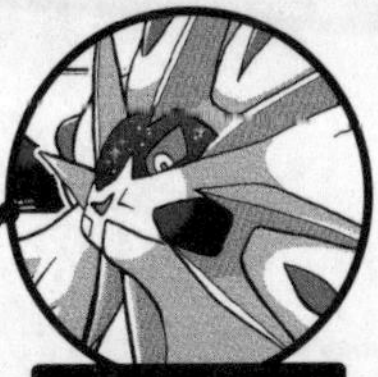

Solgaleo

Necrozma absorbed its energy, but it regained consciousness.

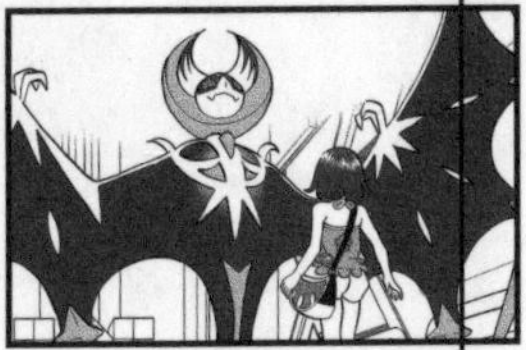

Aether Paradise

Rushed down to the lab to get Moon.

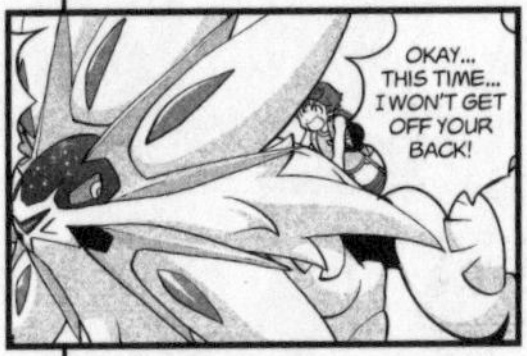
OKAY... THIS TIME... I WON'T GET OFF YOUR BACK!

Mount Lanakila

Arrived at the peak of Mount Lanakila to aid Sun in his battle.

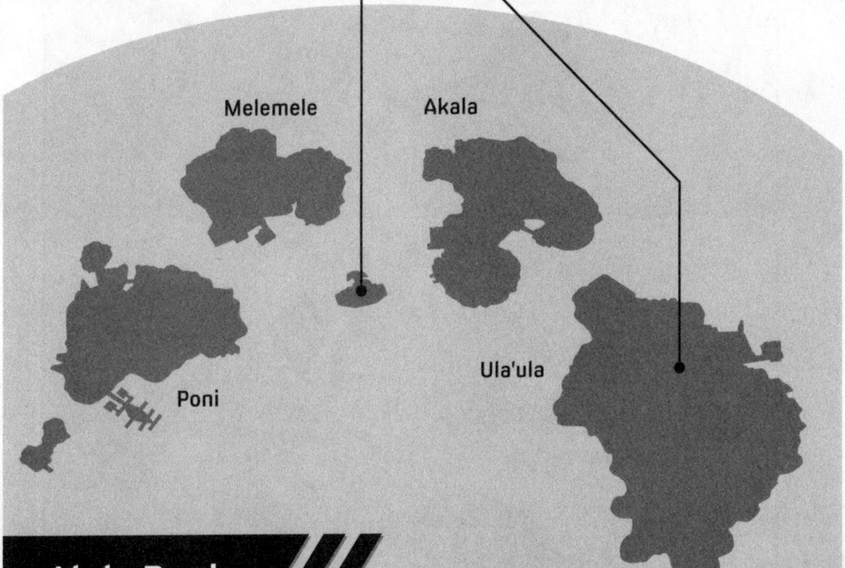
Melemele
Akala
Poni
Ula'ula

Alola Region

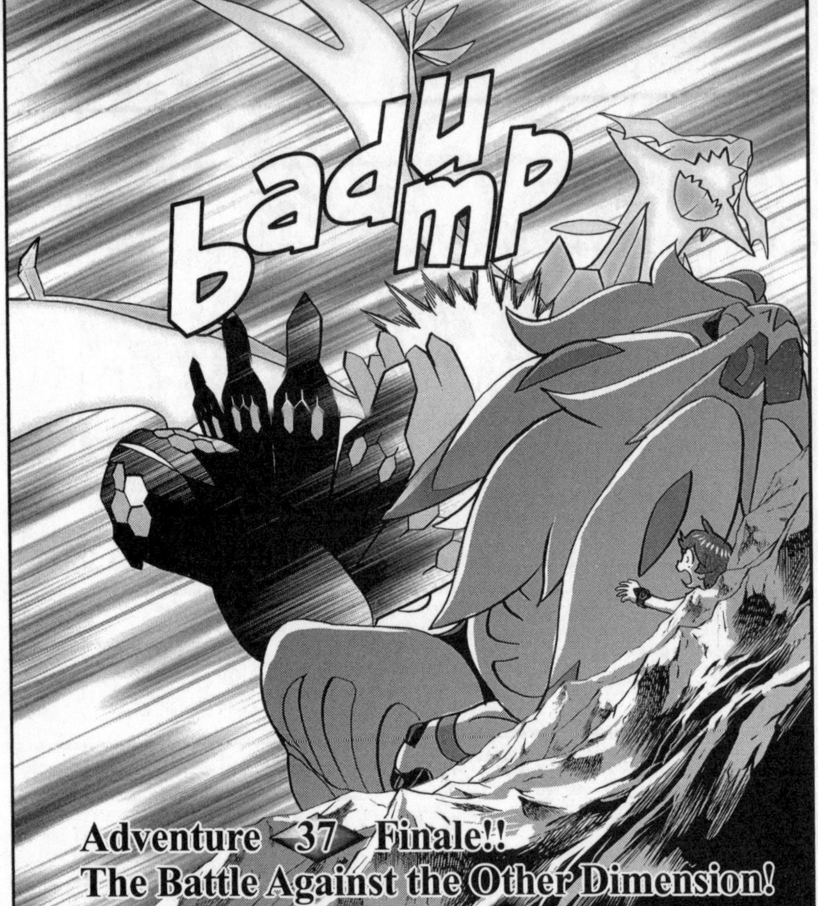
badump

Adventure 37 Finale!! The Battle Against the Other Dimension!

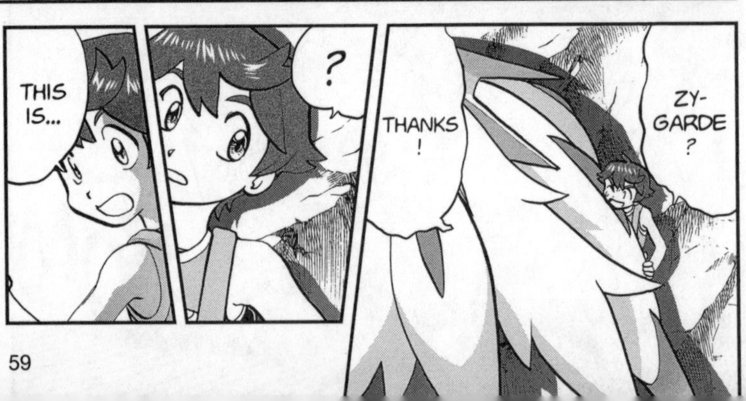
ZY-GARDE?
THANKS!
?
THIS IS...

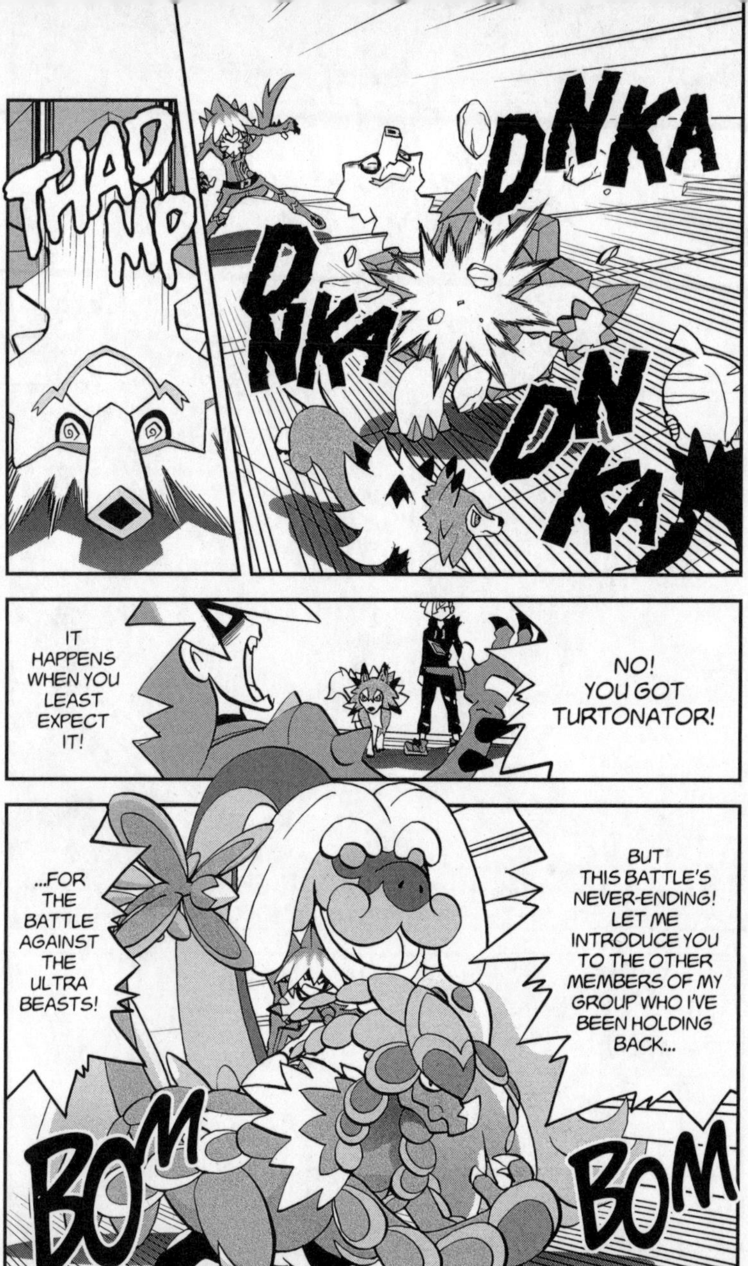
DNKA
DRKA
DNDKA
THADMP
NO! YOU GOT TURTONATOR!
IT HAPPENS WHEN YOU LEAST EXPECT IT!
BUT THIS BATTLE'S NEVER-ENDING! LET ME INTRODUCE YOU TO THE OTHER MEMBERS OF MY GROUP WHO I'VE BEEN HOLDING BACK...
...FOR THE BATTLE AGAINST THE ULTRA BEASTS!
BOM
BOM

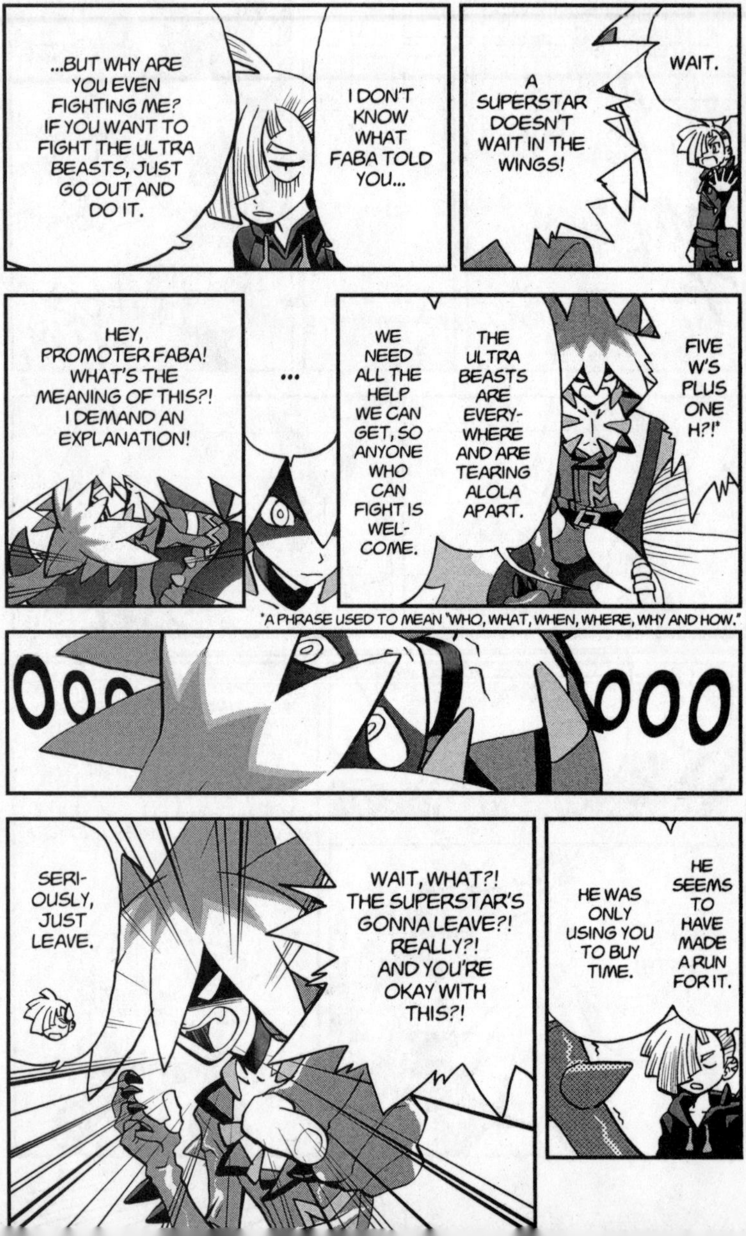
WAIT.
A SUPERSTAR DOESN'T WAIT IN THE WINGS!
I DON'T KNOW WHAT FABA TOLD YOU...
...BUT WHY ARE YOU EVEN FIGHTING ME? IF YOU WANT TO FIGHT THE ULTRA BEASTS, JUST GO OUT AND DO IT.
FIVE W'S PLUS ONE H?!*
THE ULTRA BEASTS ARE EVERYWHERE AND ARE TEARING ALOLA APART.
WE NEED ALL THE HELP WE CAN GET, SO ANYONE WHO CAN FIGHT IS WELCOME.
...
HEY, PROMOTER FABA! WHAT'S THE MEANING OF THIS?! I DEMAND AN EXPLANATION!
*A PHRASE USED TO MEAN "WHO, WHAT, WHEN, WHERE, WHY AND HOW."
OOO
OOO
HE SEEMS TO HAVE MADE A RUN FOR IT.
HE WAS ONLY USING YOU TO BUY TIME.
WAIT, WHAT?! THE SUPERSTAR'S GONNA LEAVE?! REALLY?! AND YOU'RE OKAY WITH THIS?!
SERIOUSLY, JUST LEAVE.

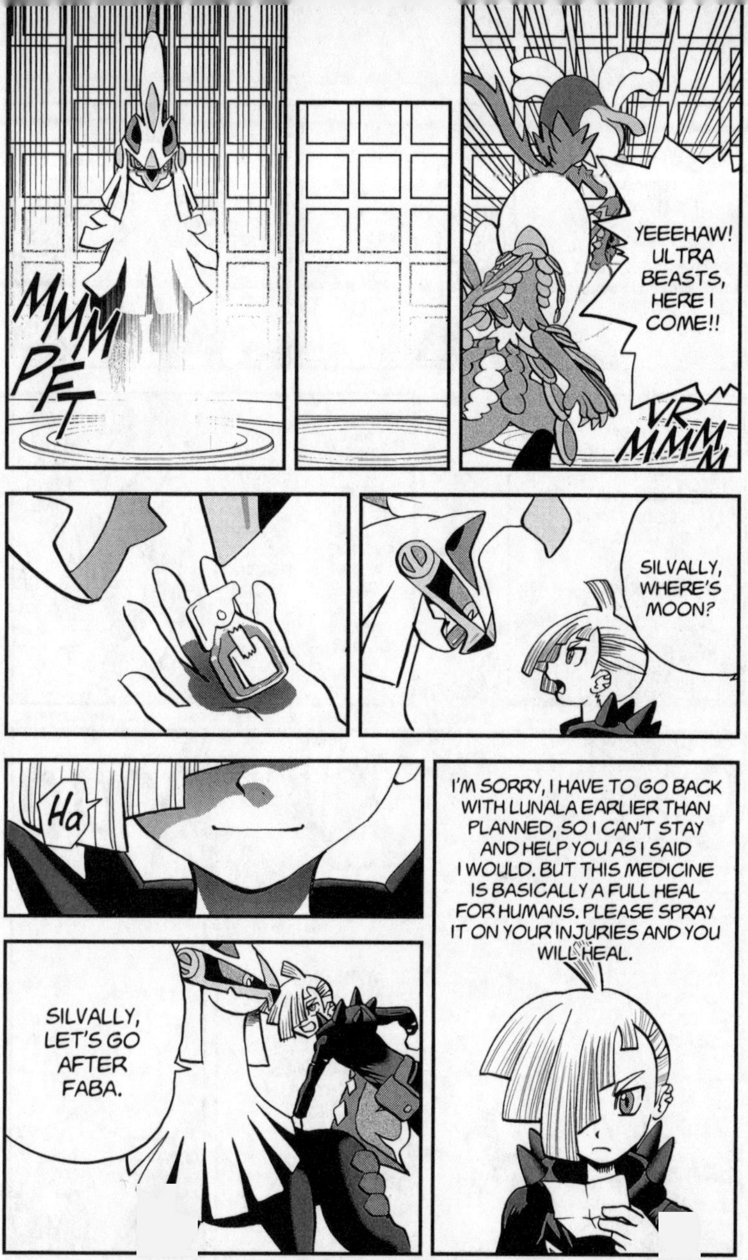
YEEEHAW! ULTRA BEASTS, HERE I COME!!
VR MMMMM
MMM PFFT
SILVALLY, WHERE'S MOON?
I'M SORRY, I HAVE TO GO BACK WITH LUNALA EARLIER THAN PLANNED, SO I CAN'T STAY AND HELP YOU AS I SAID I WOULD. BUT THIS MEDICINE IS BASICALLY A FULL HEAL FOR HUMANS. PLEASE SPRAY IT ON YOUR INJURIES AND YOU WILL HEAL.
Ha
SILVALLY, LET'S GO AFTER FABA.

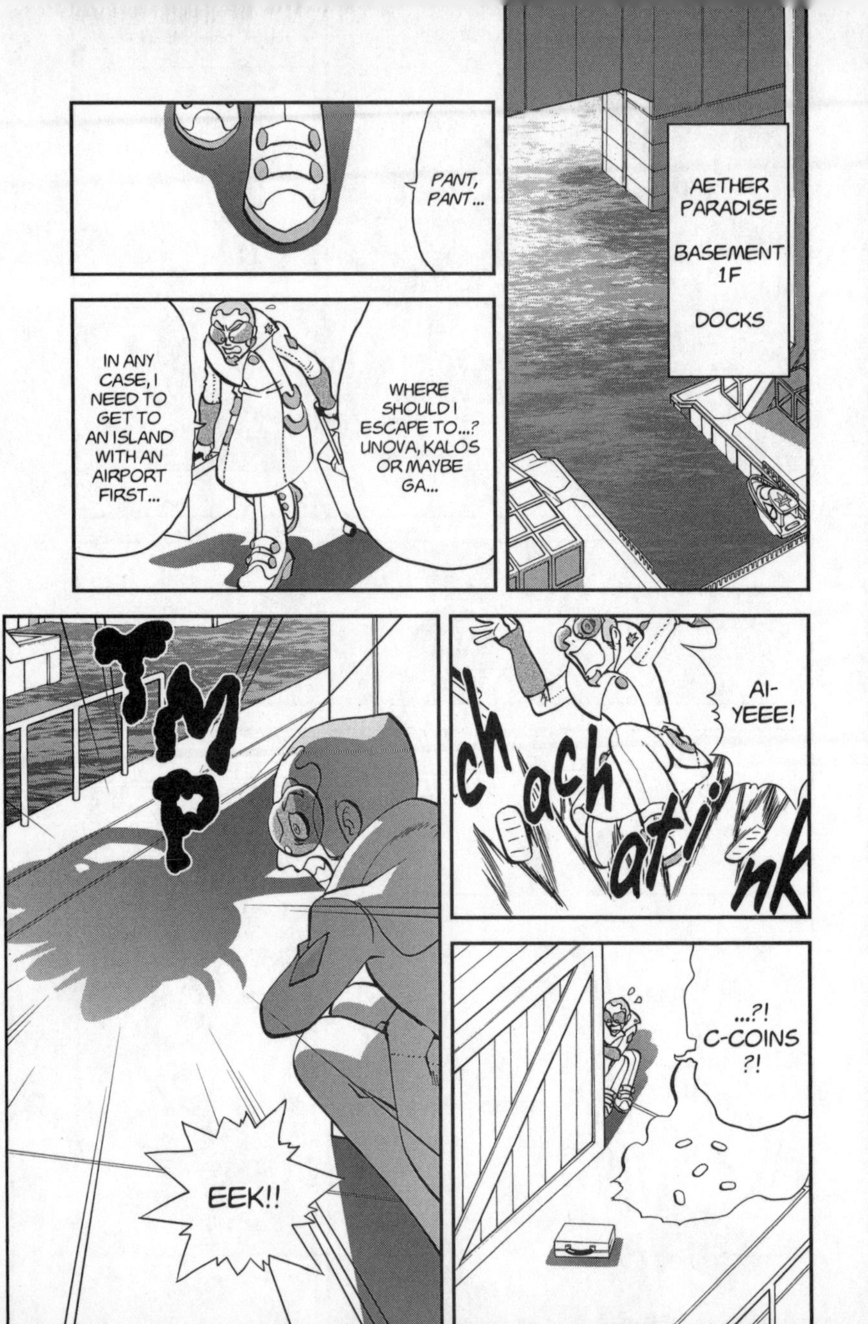
AETHER PARADISE
BASEMENT 1F
DOCKS
PANT, PANT...
WHERE SHOULD I ESCAPE TO...? UNOVA, KALOS OR MAYBE GA...
IN ANY CASE, I NEED TO GET TO AN ISLAND WITH AN AIRPORT FIRST...
AI-YEEE!
chachatink
...?! C-COINS ?!
TMP
EEK!!

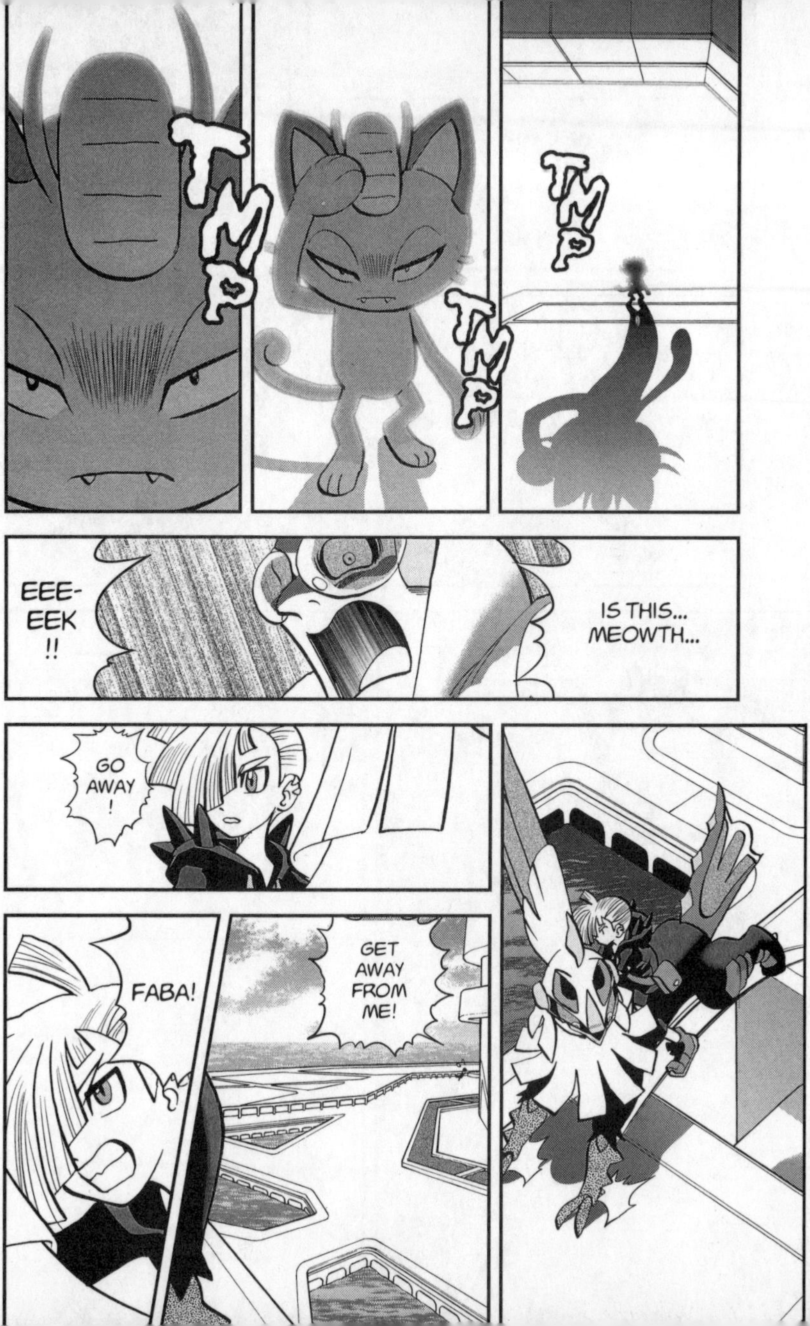
TMP
TMP
TMP
IS THIS... MEOWTH...
EEE-EEK!!
GO AWAY!
GET AWAY FROM ME!
FABA!

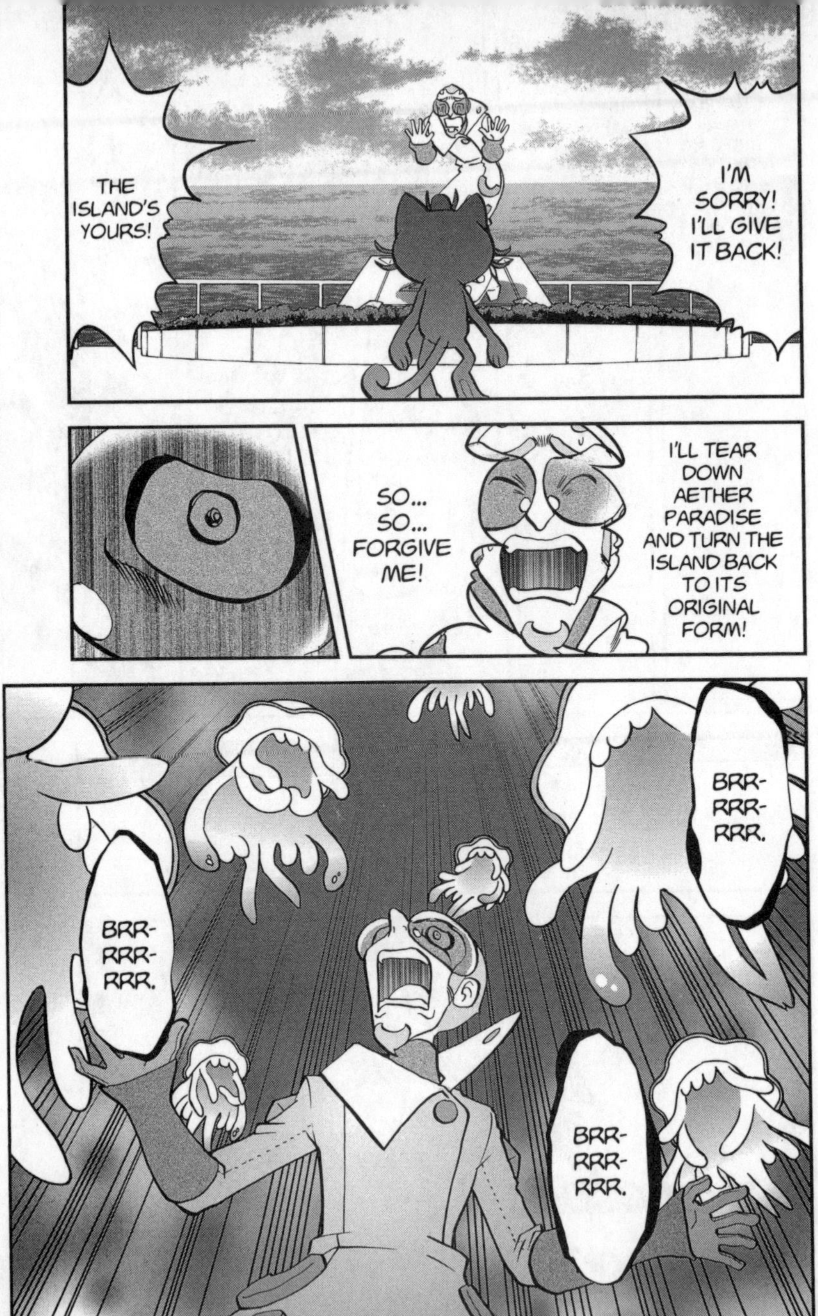
I'M SORRY! I'LL GIVE IT BACK!
THE ISLAND'S YOURS!
I'LL TEAR DOWN AETHER PARADISE AND TURN THE ISLAND BACK TO ITS ORIGINAL FORM!
SO... SO... FORGIVE ME!
BRR-RRR-RRR.
BRR-RRR-RRR.
BRR-RRR-RRR.

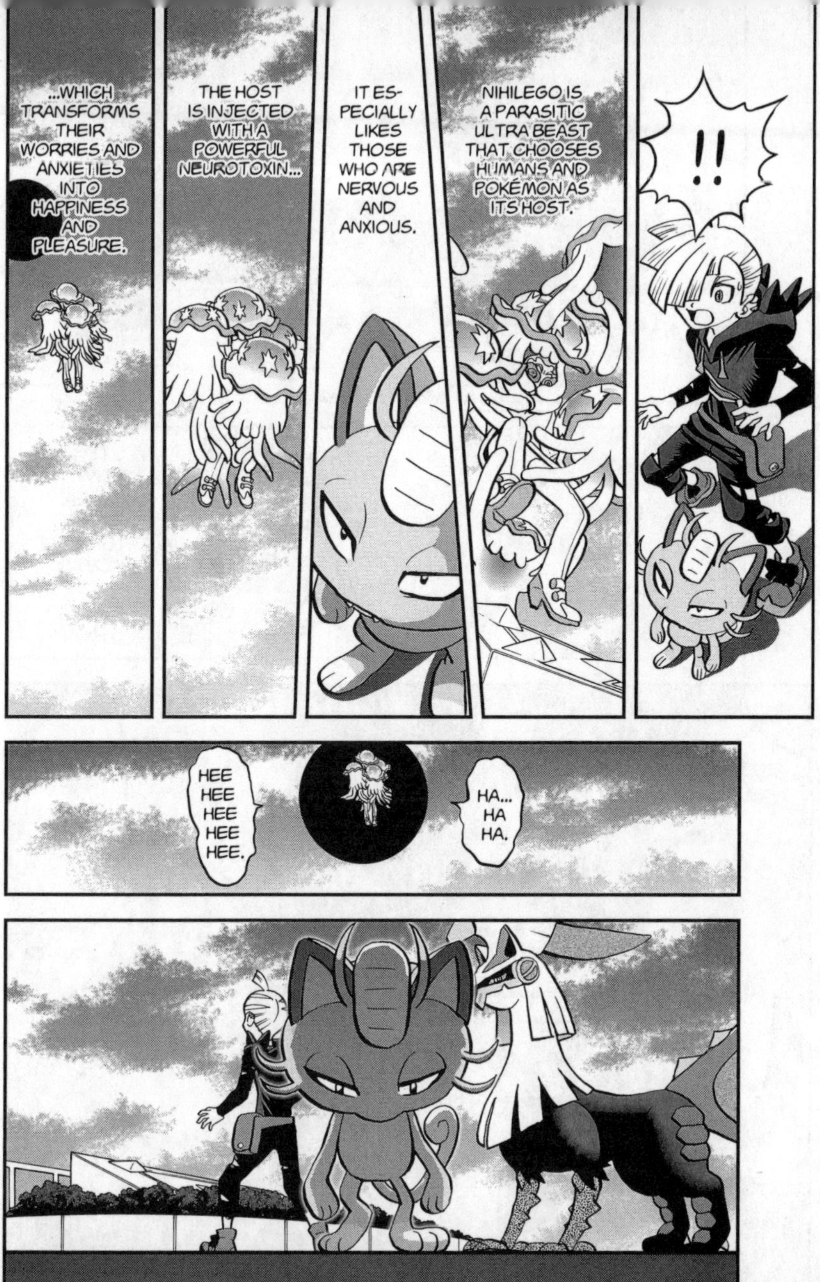
!!
NIHILEGO IS A PARASITIC ULTRA BEAST THAT CHOOSES HUMANS AND POKÉMON AS ITS HOST.
IT ES-PECIALLY LIKES THOSE WHO ARE NERVOUS AND ANXIOUS.
THE HOST IS INJECTED WITH A POWERFUL NEUROTOXIN...
...WHICH TRANSFORMS THEIR WORRIES AND ANXIETIES INTO HAPPINESS AND PLEASURE.
HA... HA HA.
HEE HEE HEE HEE HEE.

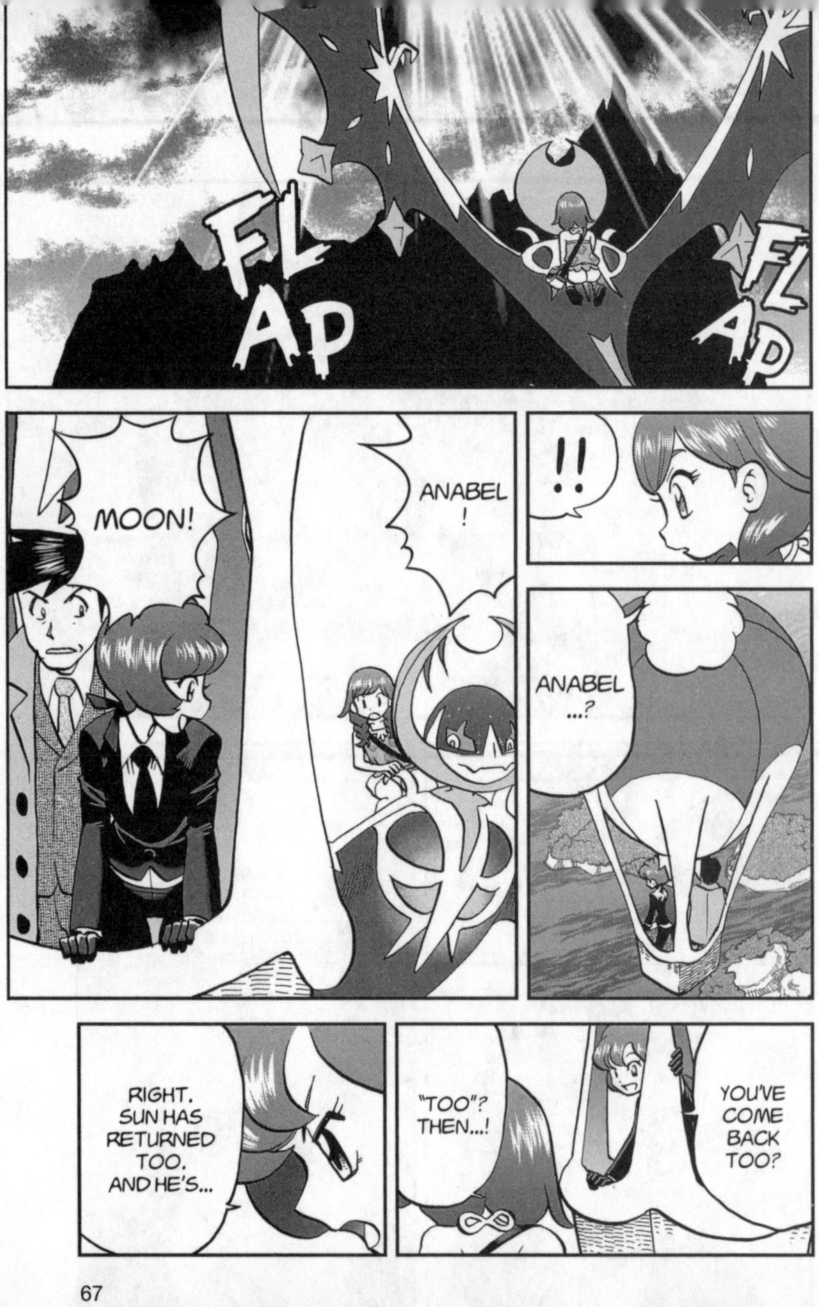
FLAP
FLAP
!!
ANABEL ...?
ANABEL !
MOON!
YOU'VE COME BACK TOO?
"TOO"? THEN...!
RIGHT. SUN HAS RETURNED TOO. AND HE'S...

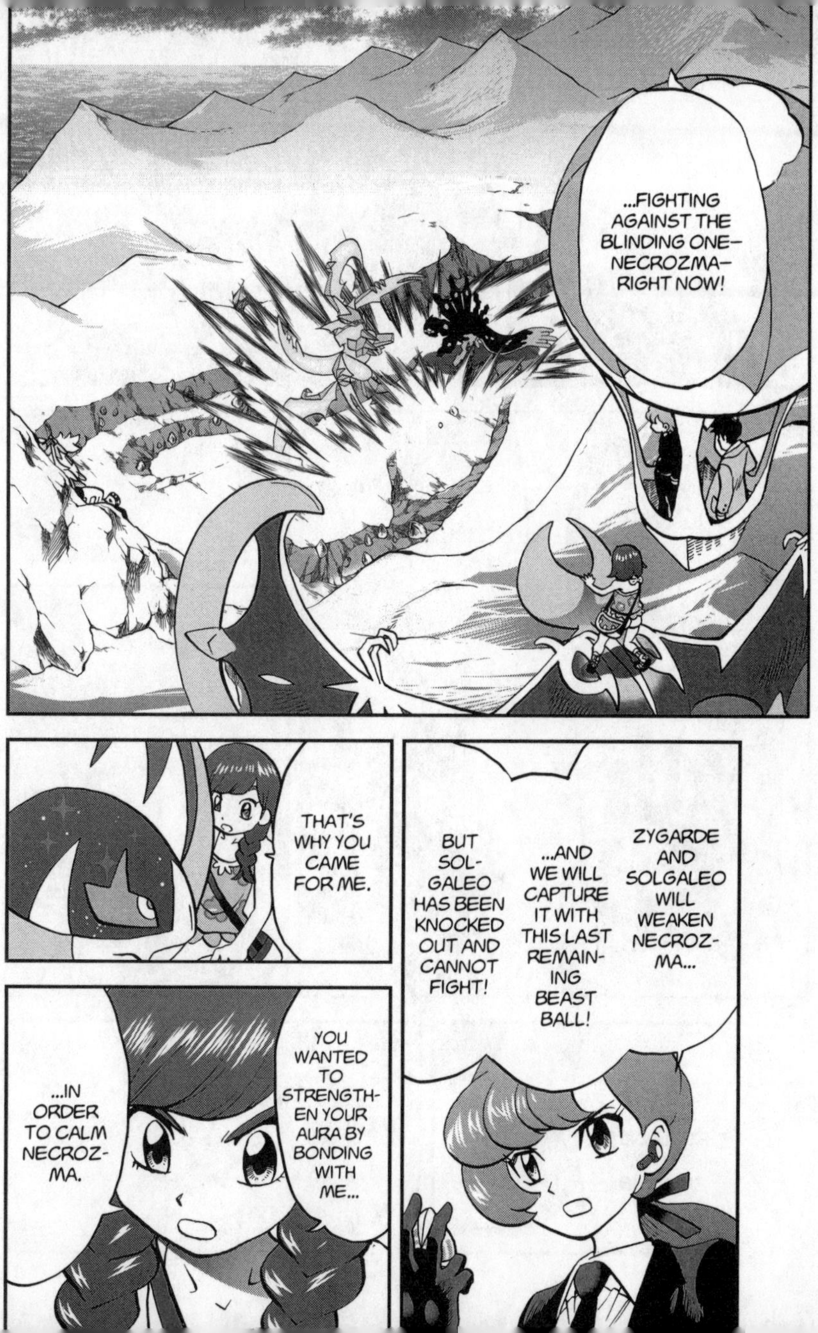
...FIGHTING AGAINST THE BLINDING ONE—NECROZMA—RIGHT NOW!
ZYGARDE AND SOLGALEO WILL WEAKEN NECROZ-MA...
...AND WE WILL CAPTURE IT WITH THIS LAST REMAIN-ING BEAST BALL!
BUT SOL-GALEO HAS BEEN KNOCKED OUT AND CANNOT FIGHT!
THAT'S WHY YOU CAME FOR ME.
YOU WANTED TO STRENGTH-EN YOUR AURA BY BONDING WITH ME...
...IN ORDER TO CALM NECROZ-MA.

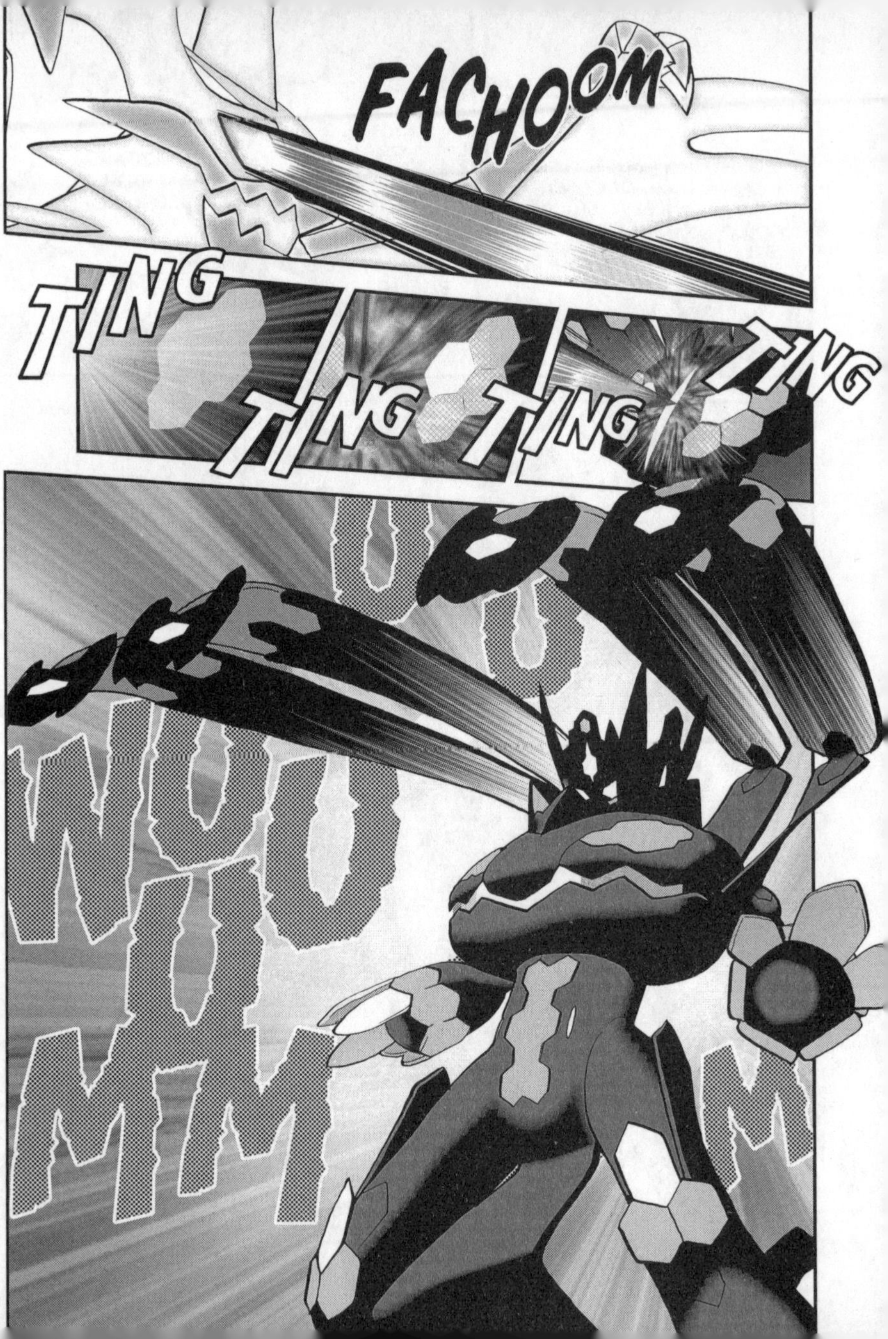
FACHOOM
TING
TING
TING
TING
WUUUUUMMM

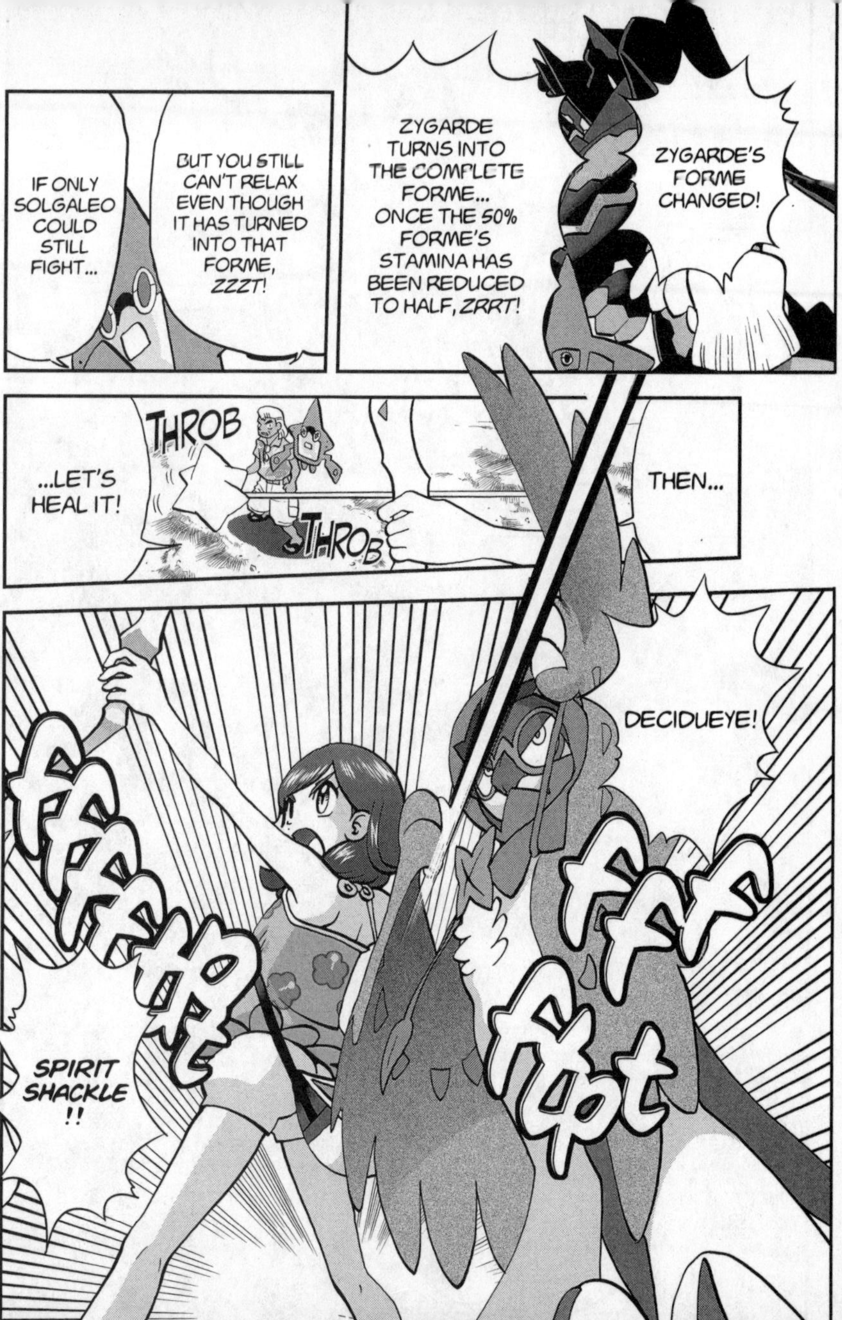
ZYGARDE'S FORME CHANGED!
ZYGARDE TURNS INTO THE COMPLETE FORME... ONCE THE 50% FORME'S STAMINA HAS BEEN REDUCED TO HALF, ZRRT!
BUT YOU STILL CAN'T RELAX EVEN THOUGH IT HAS TURNED INTO THAT FORME, ZZZT!
IF ONLY SOLGALEO COULD STILL FIGHT...
THEN...
THROB
THROB
...LET'S HEAL IT!
DECIDUEYE!
SPIRIT SHACKLE!!

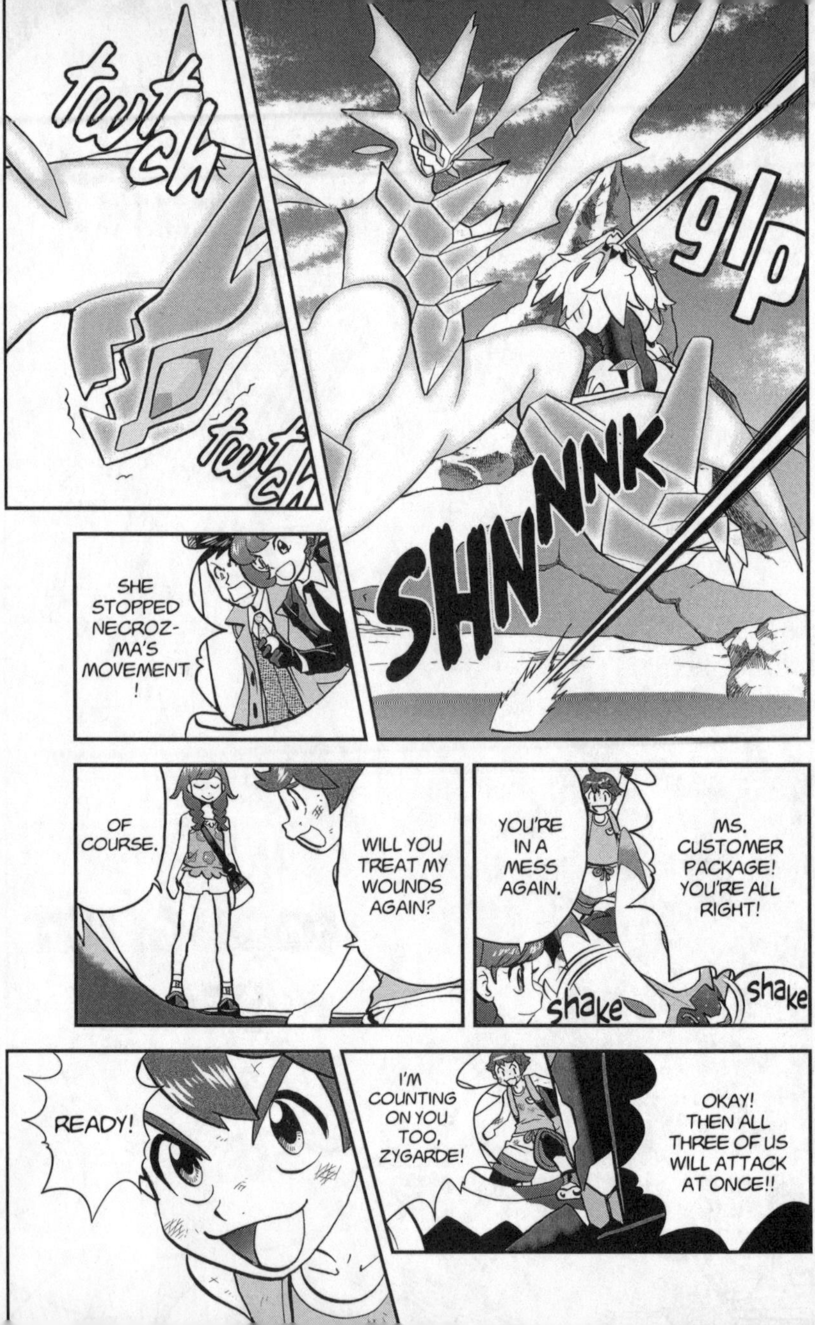
glp
SHNNNK
twitch
twitch
SHE STOPPED NECROZ-MA'S MOVEMENT!
MS. CUSTOMER PACKAGE! YOU'RE ALL RIGHT!
YOU'RE IN A MESS AGAIN.
shake
shake
WILL YOU TREAT MY WOUNDS AGAIN?
OF COURSE.
OKAY! THEN ALL THREE OF US WILL ATTACK AT ONCE!!
I'M COUNTING ON YOU TOO, ZYGARDE!
READY!

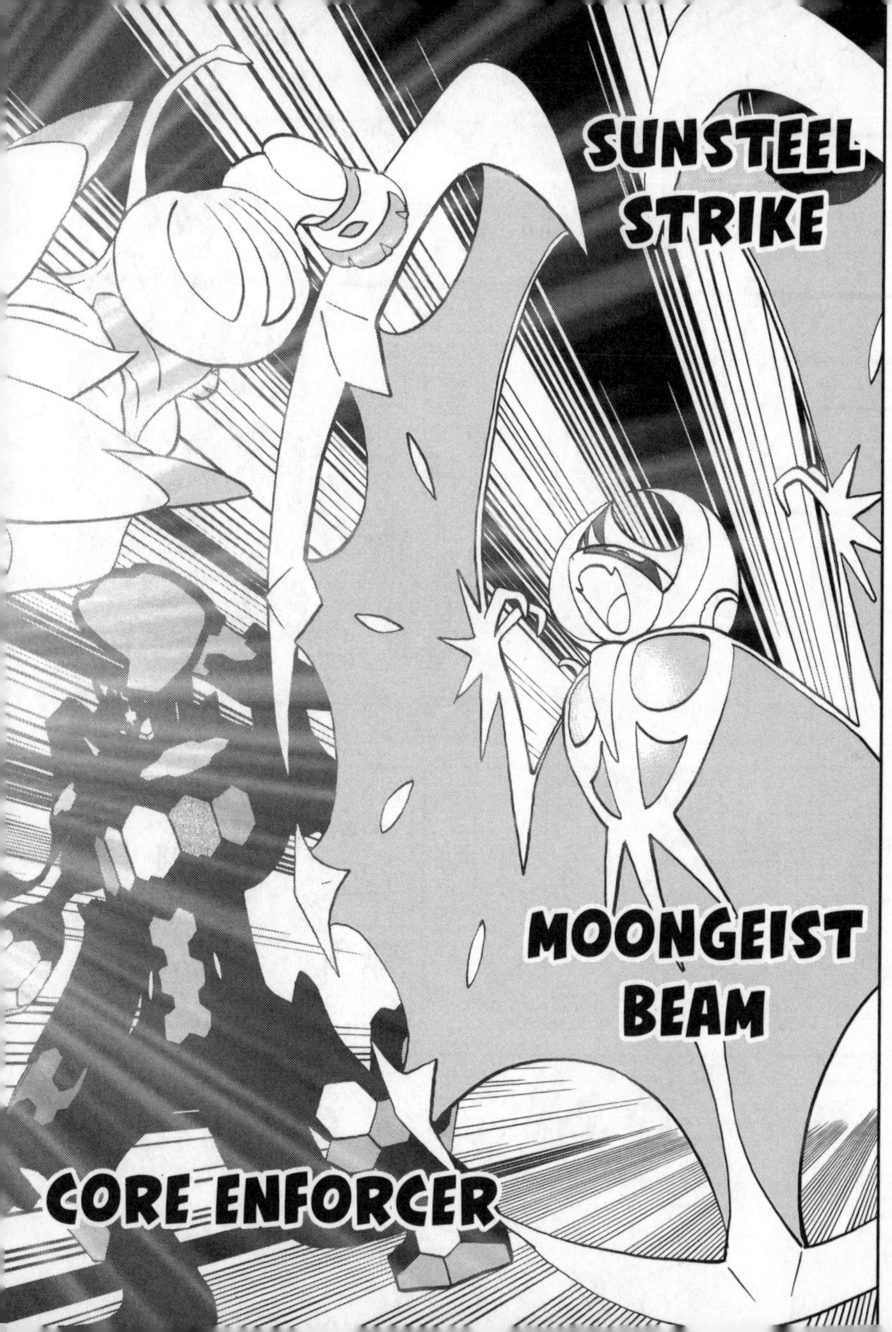
SUNSTEEL STRIKE
MOONGEIST BEAM
CORE ENFORCER

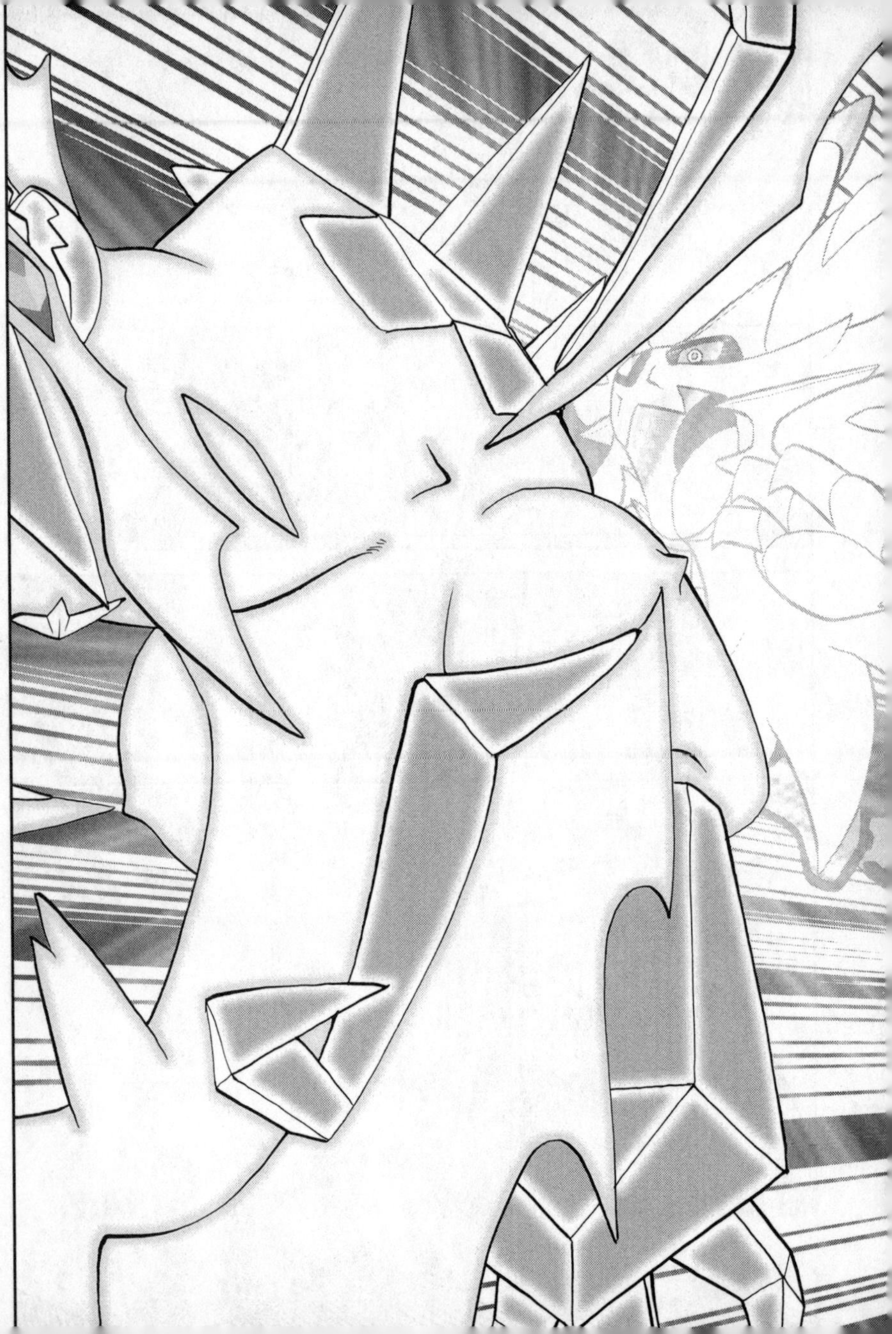

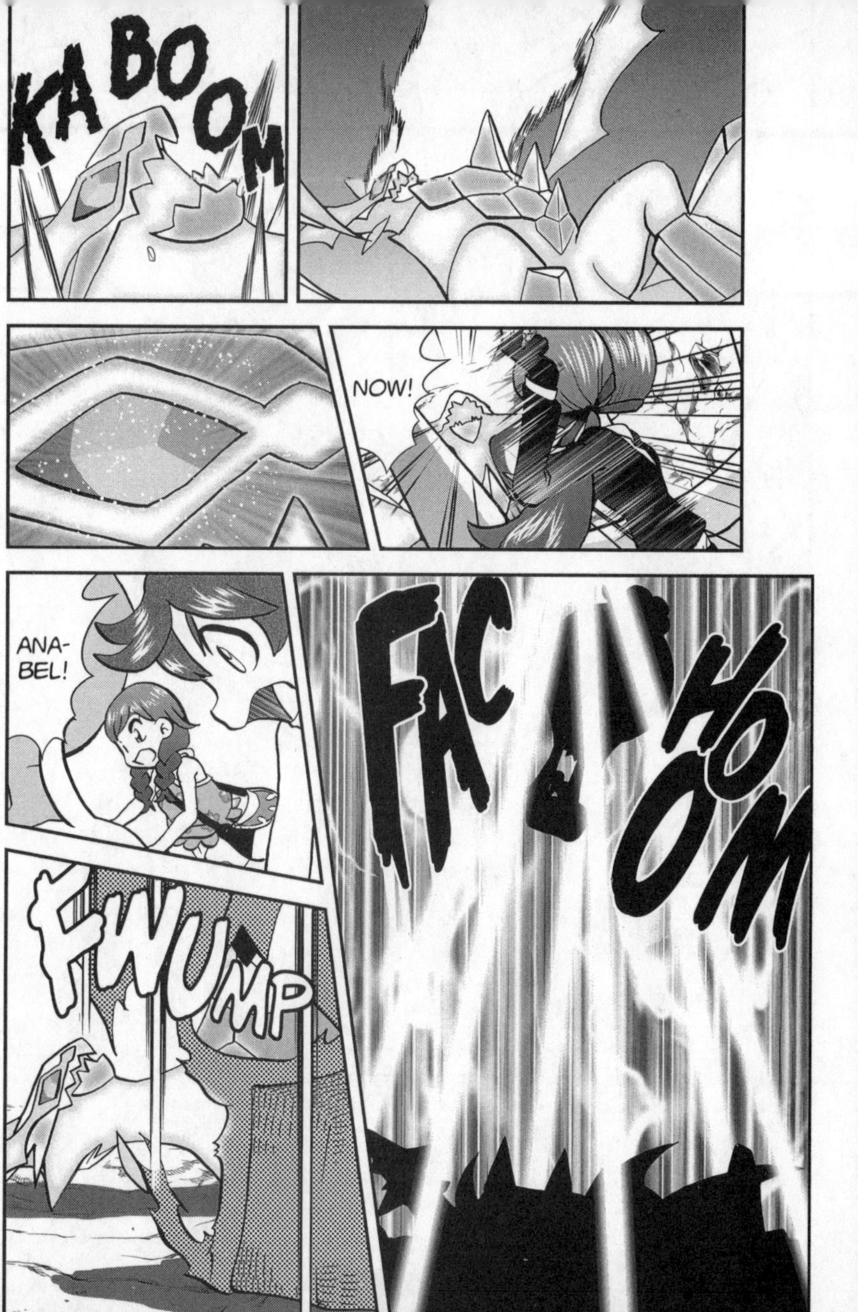
KABOOM
NOW!
ANA-
BEL!
FWUMP

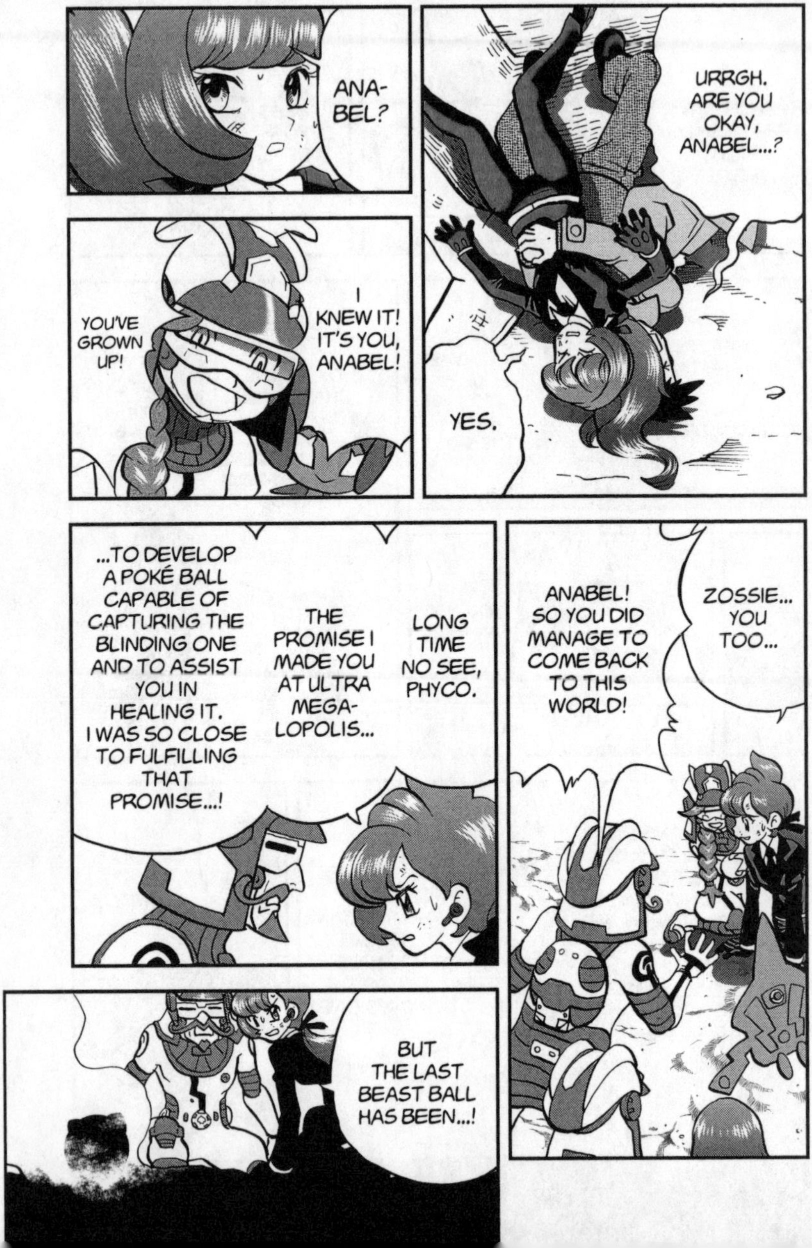
URRGH. ARE YOU OKAY, ANABEL...?
YES.
ANA-BEL?
I KNEW IT! IT'S YOU, ANABEL!
YOU'VE GROWN UP!
ZOSSIE... YOU TOO...
ANABEL! SO YOU DID MANAGE TO COME BACK TO THIS WORLD!
LONG TIME NO SEE, PHYCO.
THE PROMISE I MADE YOU AT ULTRA MEGA-LOPOLIS...
...TO DEVELOP A POKÉ BALL CAPABLE OF CAPTURING THE BLINDING ONE AND TO ASSIST YOU IN HEALING IT. I WAS SO CLOSE TO FULFILLING THAT PROMISE...!
BUT THE LAST BEAST BALL HAS BEEN...!

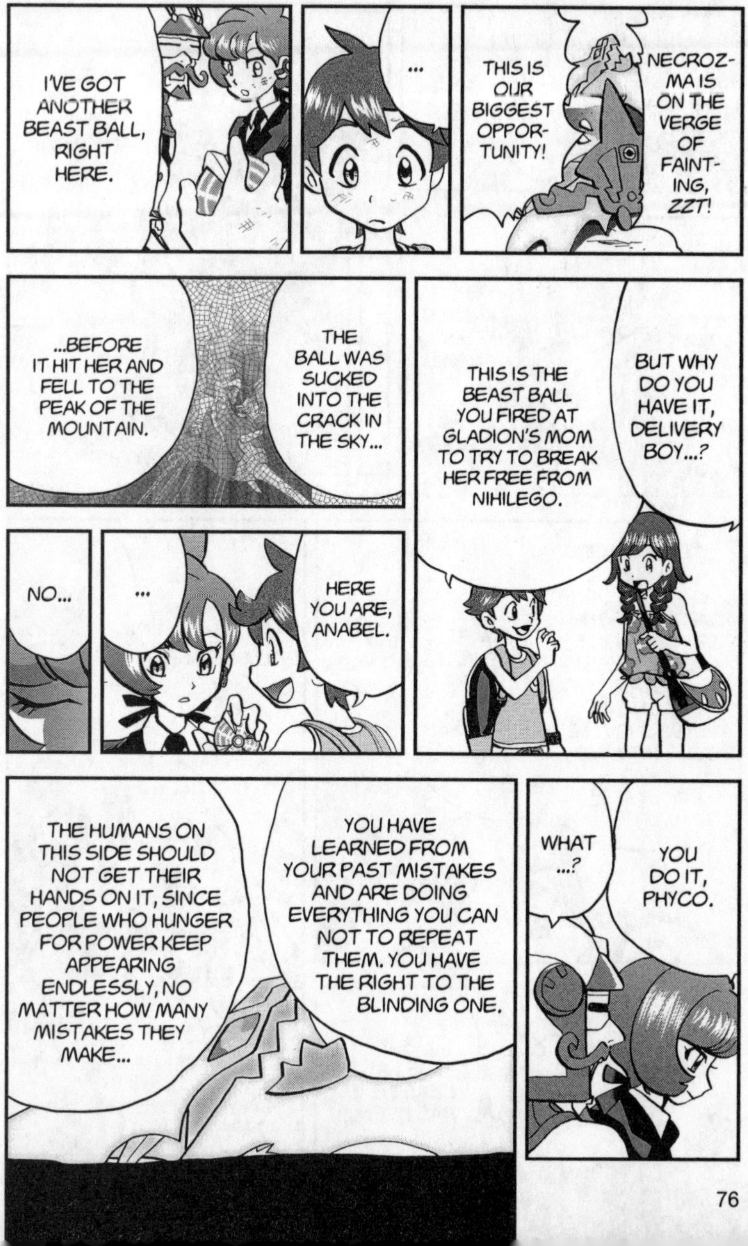
NECROZMA IS ON THE VERGE OF FAINTING, ZZT!
THIS IS OUR BIGGEST OPPORTUNITY!
...
I'VE GOT ANOTHER BEAST BALL, RIGHT HERE.
BUT WHY DO YOU HAVE IT, DELIVERY BOY...?
THIS IS THE BEAST BALL YOU FIRED AT GLADION'S MOM TO TRY TO BREAK HER FREE FROM NIHILEGO.
THE BALL WAS SUCKED INTO THE CRACK IN THE SKY...
...BEFORE IT HIT HER AND FELL TO THE PEAK OF THE MOUNTAIN.
HERE YOU ARE, ANABEL.
...
NO...
YOU DO IT, PHYCO.
WHAT ...?
YOU HAVE LEARNED FROM YOUR PAST MISTAKES AND ARE DOING EVERYTHING YOU CAN NOT TO REPEAT THEM. YOU HAVE THE RIGHT TO THE BLINDING ONE.
THE HUMANS ON THIS SIDE SHOULD NOT GET THEIR HANDS ON IT, SINCE PEOPLE WHO HUNGER FOR POWER KEEP APPEARING ENDLESSLY, NO MATTER HOW MANY MISTAKES THEY MAKE...

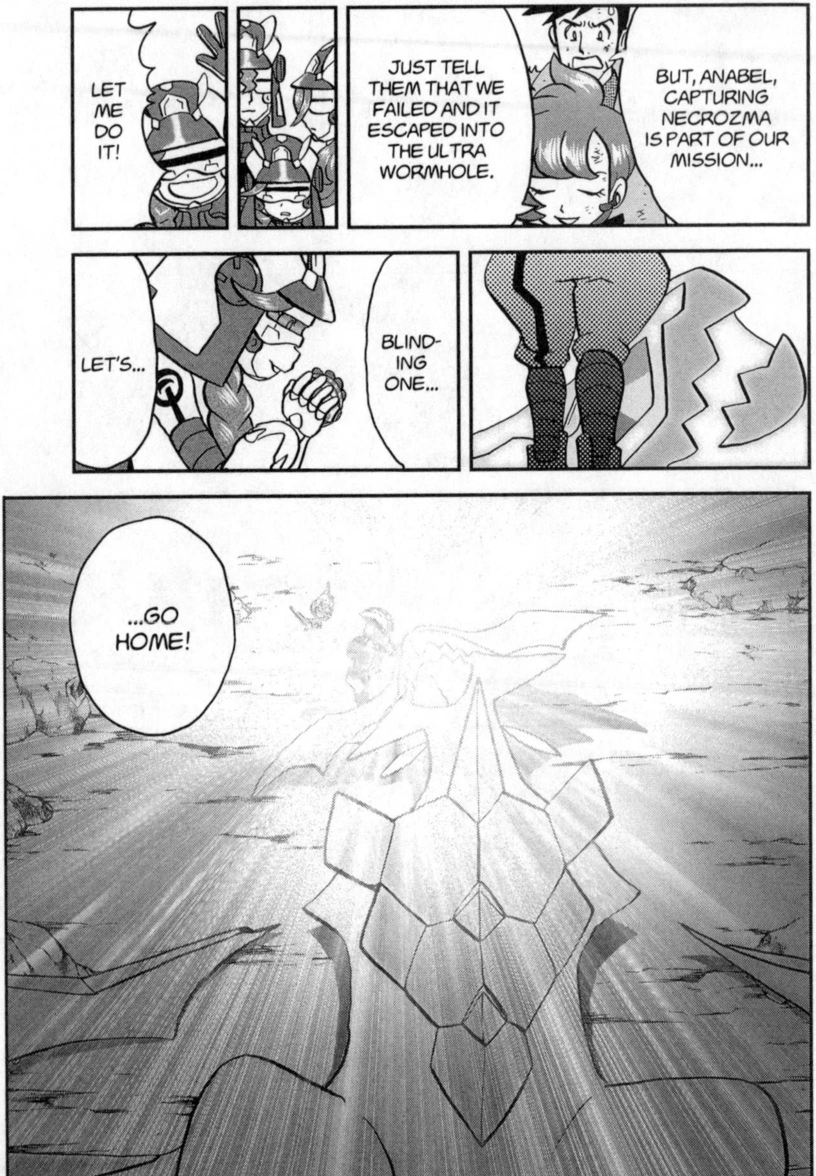
BUT, ANABEL, CAPTURING NECROZMA IS PART OF OUR MISSION...
JUST TELL THEM THAT WE FAILED AND IT ESCAPED INTO THE ULTRA WORMHOLE.
LET ME DO IT!
BLINDING ONE...
LET'S...
...GO HOME!

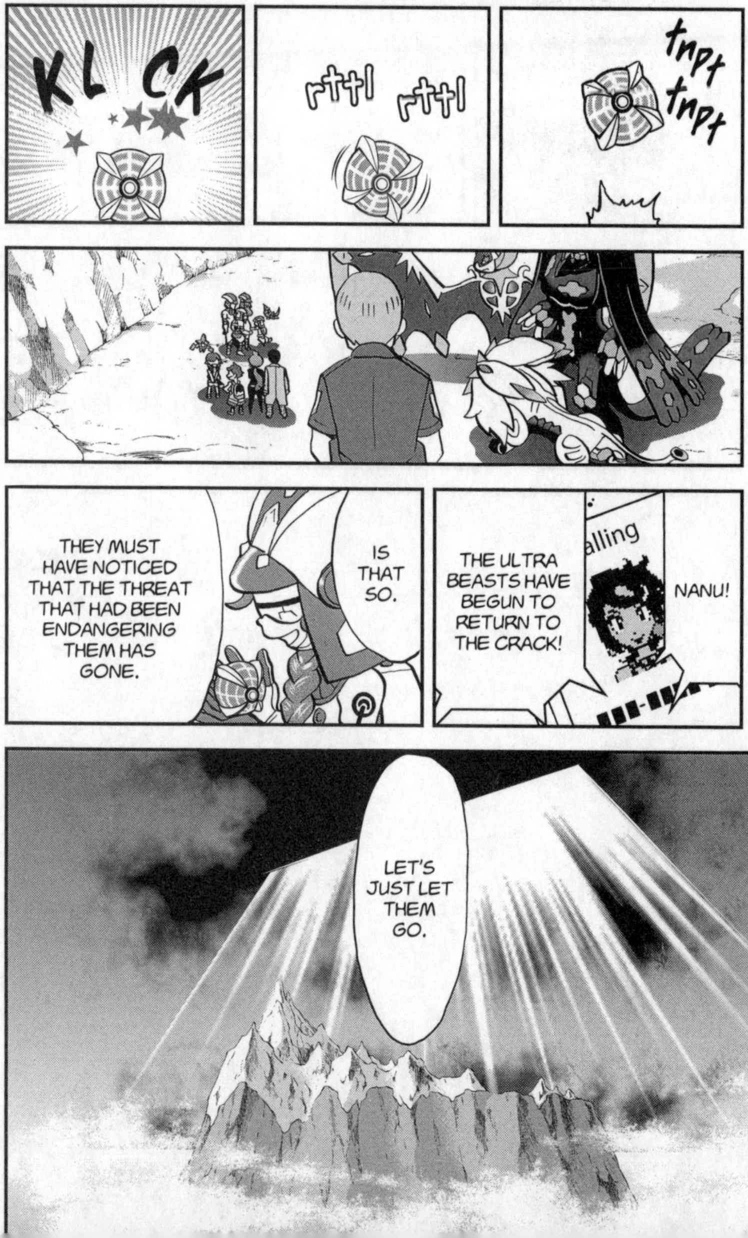
tnpt tnpt
rttl rttl
KLCK
alling
NANU!
THE ULTRA BEASTS HAVE BEGUN TO RETURN TO THE CRACK!
IS THAT SO.
THEY MUST HAVE NOTICED THAT THE THREAT THAT HAD BEEN ENDANGERING THEM HAS GONE.
LET'S JUST LET THEM GO.

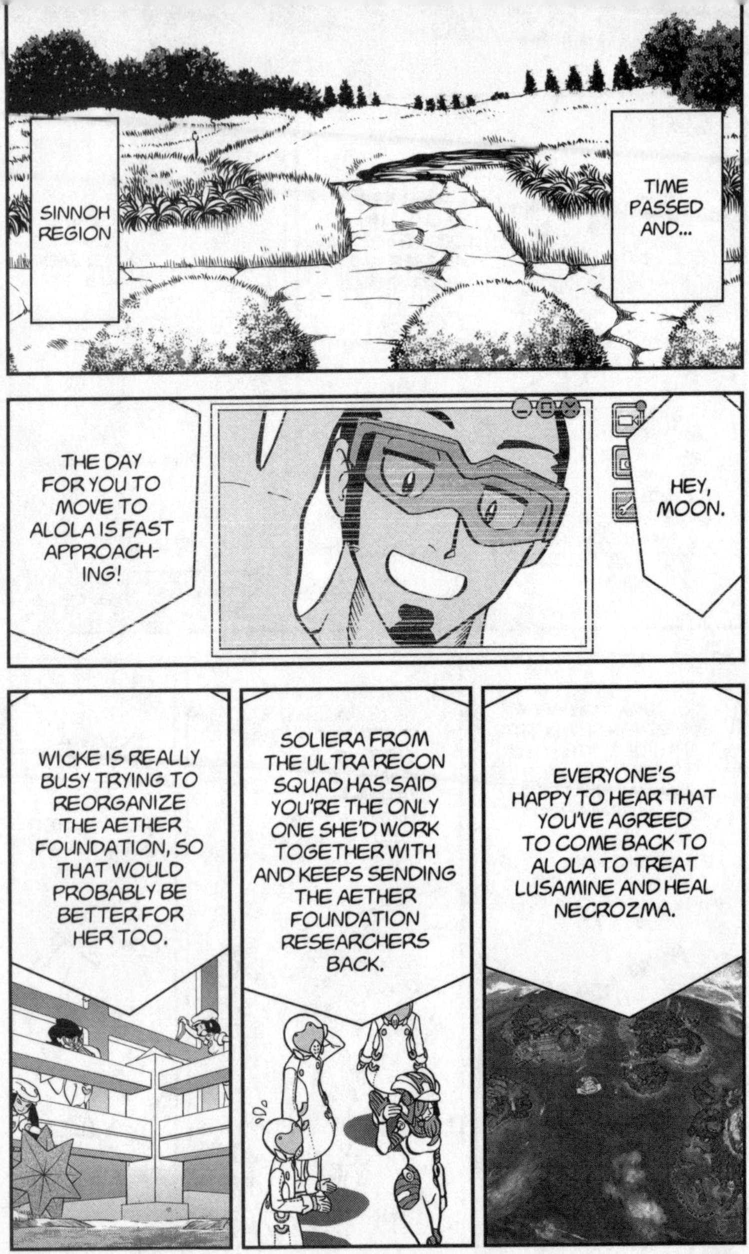
TIME PASSED AND...
SINNOH REGION
HEY, MOON.
THE DAY FOR YOU TO MOVE TO ALOLA IS FAST APPROACH-ING!
EVERYONE'S HAPPY TO HEAR THAT YOU'VE AGREED TO COME BACK TO ALOLA TO TREAT LUSAMINE AND HEAL NECROZMA.
SOLIERA FROM THE ULTRA RECON SQUAD HAS SAID YOU'RE THE ONLY ONE SHE'D WORK TOGETHER WITH AND KEEPS SENDING THE AETHER FOUNDATION RESEARCHERS BACK.
WICKE IS REALLY BUSY TRYING TO REORGANIZE THE AETHER FOUNDATION, SO THAT WOULD PROBABLY BE BETTER FOR HER TOO.

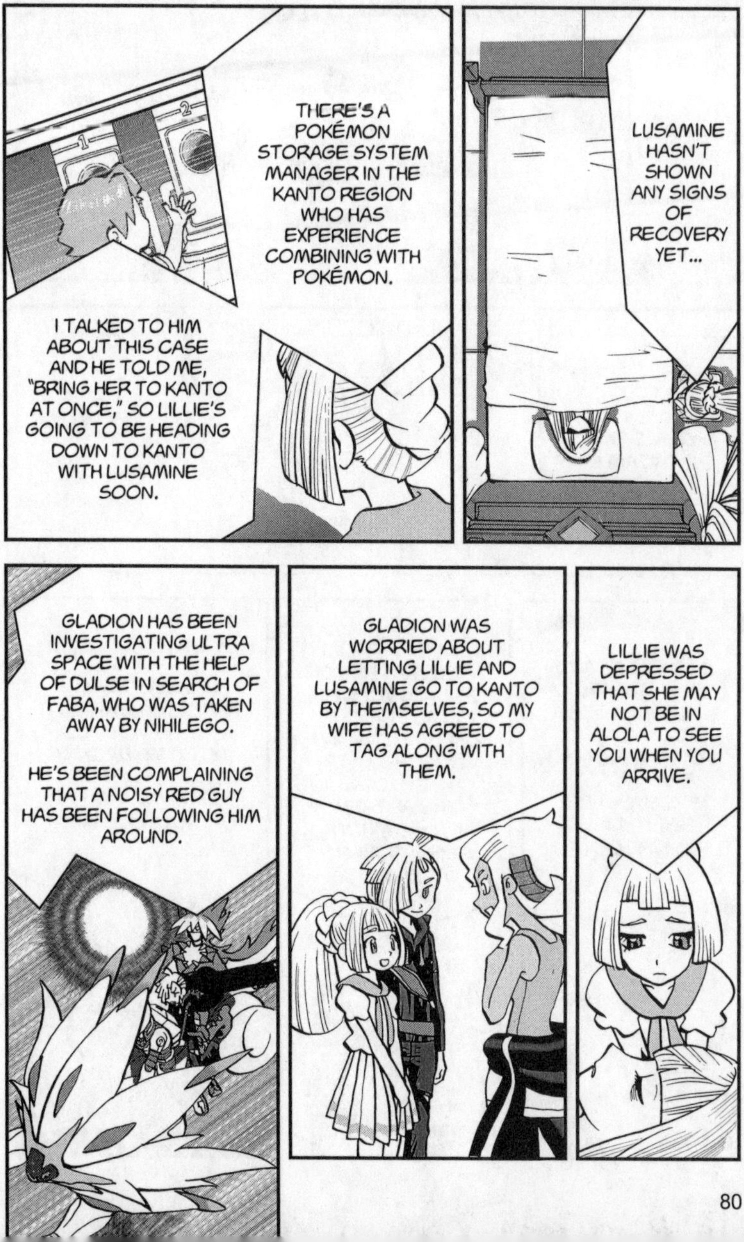
LUSAMINE HASN'T SHOWN ANY SIGNS OF RECOVERY YET...
THERE'S A POKÉMON STORAGE SYSTEM MANAGER IN THE KANTO REGION WHO HAS EXPERIENCE COMBINING WITH POKÉMON.
I TALKED TO HIM ABOUT THIS CASE AND HE TOLD ME, "BRING HER TO KANTO AT ONCE," SO LILLIE'S GOING TO BE HEADING DOWN TO KANTO WITH LUSAMINE SOON.
LILLIE WAS DEPRESSED THAT SHE MAY NOT BE IN ALOLA TO SEE YOU WHEN YOU ARRIVE.
GLADION WAS WORRIED ABOUT LETTING LILLIE AND LUSAMINE GO TO KANTO BY THEMSELVES, SO MY WIFE HAS AGREED TO TAG ALONG WITH THEM.
GLADION HAS BEEN INVESTIGATING ULTRA SPACE WITH THE HELP OF DULSE IN SEARCH OF FABA, WHO WAS TAKEN AWAY BY NIHILEGO.
HE'S BEEN COMPLAINING THAT A NOISY RED GUY HAS BEEN FOLLOWING HIM AROUND.

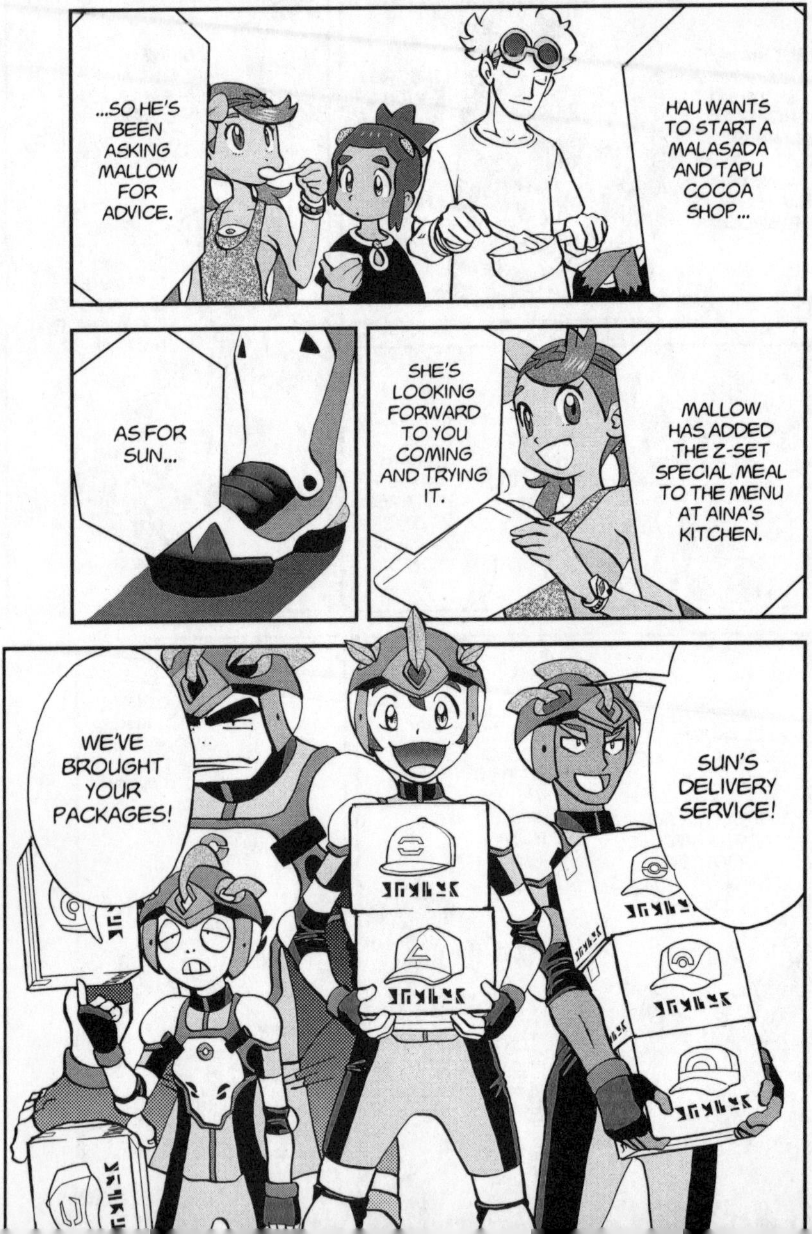
HAU WANTS TO START A MALASADA AND TAPU COCOA SHOP...
...SO HE'S BEEN ASKING MALLOW FOR ADVICE.
MALLOW HAS ADDED THE Z-SET SPECIAL MEAL TO THE MENU AT AINA'S KITCHEN.
SHE'S LOOKING FORWARD TO YOU COMING AND TRYING IT.
AS FOR SUN...
SUN'S DELIVERY SERVICE!
WE'VE BROUGHT YOUR PACKAGES!

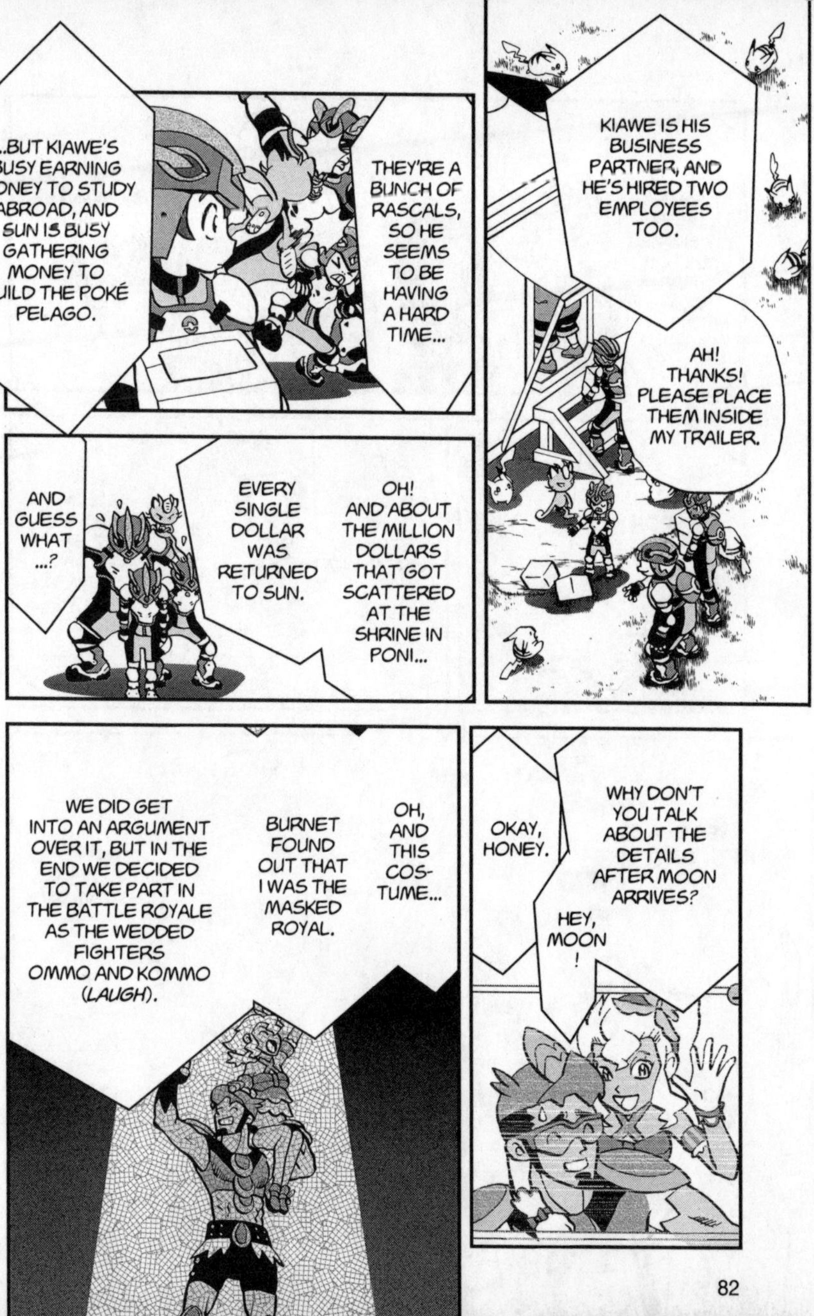
KIAWE IS HIS BUSINESS PARTNER, AND HE'S HIRED TWO EMPLOYEES TOO.
AH! THANKS! PLEASE PLACE THEM INSIDE MY TRAILER.
THEY'RE A BUNCH OF RASCALS, SO HE SEEMS TO BE HAVING A HARD TIME...
...BUT KIAWE'S BUSY EARNING MONEY TO STUDY ABROAD, AND SUN IS BUSY GATHERING MONEY TO BUILD THE POKÉ PELAGO.
OH! AND ABOUT THE MILLION DOLLARS THAT GOT SCATTERED AT THE SHRINE IN PONI...
EVERY SINGLE DOLLAR WAS RETURNED TO SUN.
AND GUESS WHAT ...?
WHY DON'T YOU TALK ABOUT THE DETAILS AFTER MOON ARRIVES?
OKAY, HONEY.
HEY, MOON!
OH, AND THIS COSTUME...
BURNET FOUND OUT THAT I WAS THE MASKED ROYAL.
WE DID GET INTO AN ARGUMENT OVER IT, BUT IN THE END WE DECIDED TO TAKE PART IN THE BATTLE ROYALE AS THE WEDDED FIGHTERS OMMO AND KOMMO (*LAUGH*).

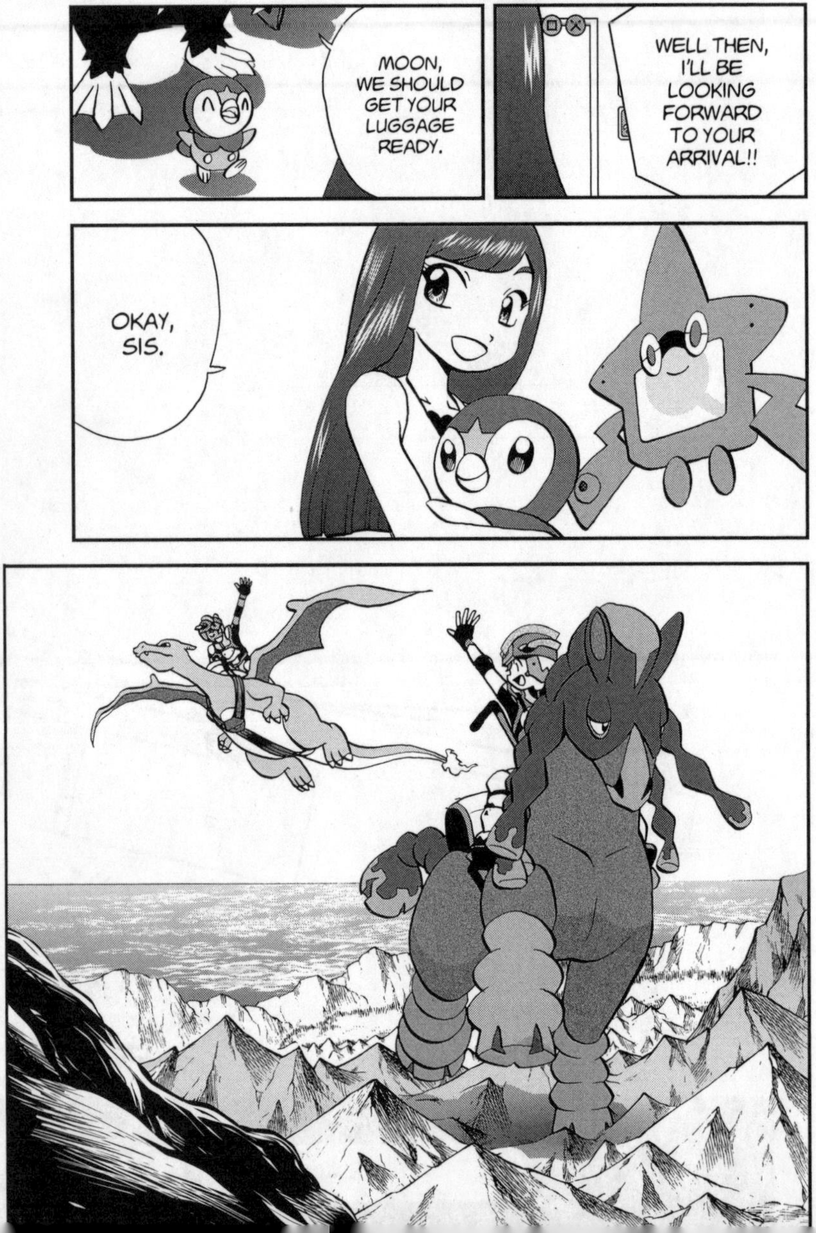
WELL THEN, I'LL BE LOOKING FORWARD TO YOUR ARRIVAL!!
MOON, WE SHOULD GET YOUR LUGGAGE READY.
OKAY, SIS.

Delivery Slip
SENDING ADDRESS
NAME
Time of Delivery:
ITEMS
8:00–10:00
10:00–12:00
12:00–14:00
14:00–16:00
16:00–18:00
18:00–20:00
Breakable
Perishable
Fragile
Hazardous
THE END

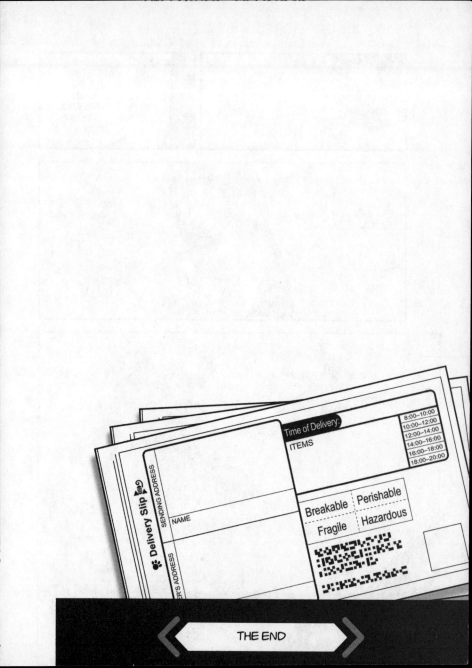

POKÉMON™
SUN & MOON

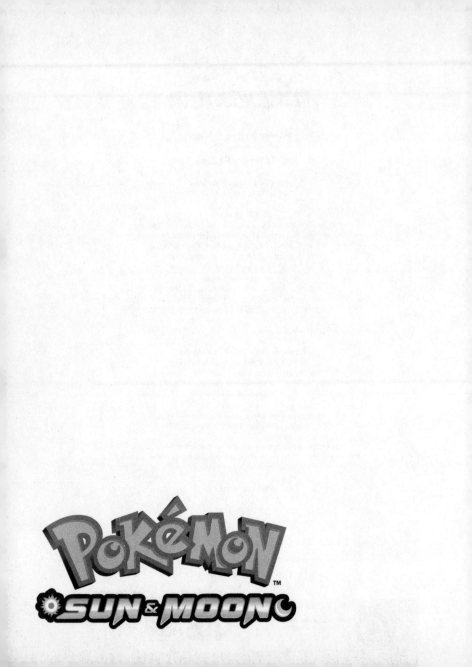

Pokémon Sun & Moon
Volume 12
VIZ Media Edition

Story by HIDENORI KUSAKA
Art by SATOSHI YAMAMOTO

©2022 Pokémon.
©1995–2020 Nintendo / Creatures Inc. / GAME FREAK inc.
TM, ®, and character names are trademarks of Nintendo.
POCKET MONSTERS SPECIAL SUN • MOON Vol. 6
by Hidenori KUSAKA, Satoshi YAMAMOTO
© 2017 Hidenori KUSAKA, Satoshi YAMAMOTO
All rights reserved.
Original Japanese edition published by SHOGAKUKAN.
English translation rights in the United States of America, Canada, the United Kingdom,
Ireland, Australia and New Zealand arranged with SHOGAKUKAN.

Original Cover Design—Hiroyuki KAWASOME (grafio)

Translation—Tetsuichiro Miyaki
English Adaptation—Bryant Turnage
Touch-Up & Lettering—Susan Daigle-Leach
Design—Alice Lewis
Editor—Joel Enos

Printed in the U.S.A.

Published by
VIZ Media, LLC
P.O. Box 77010
San Francisco, CA 94107

10 9 8 7 6 5 4 3 2 1
First printing, January 2022

PARENTAL ADVISORY
POKÉMON: SUN & MOON is rated A
and is suitable for readers of all ages.

viz.com

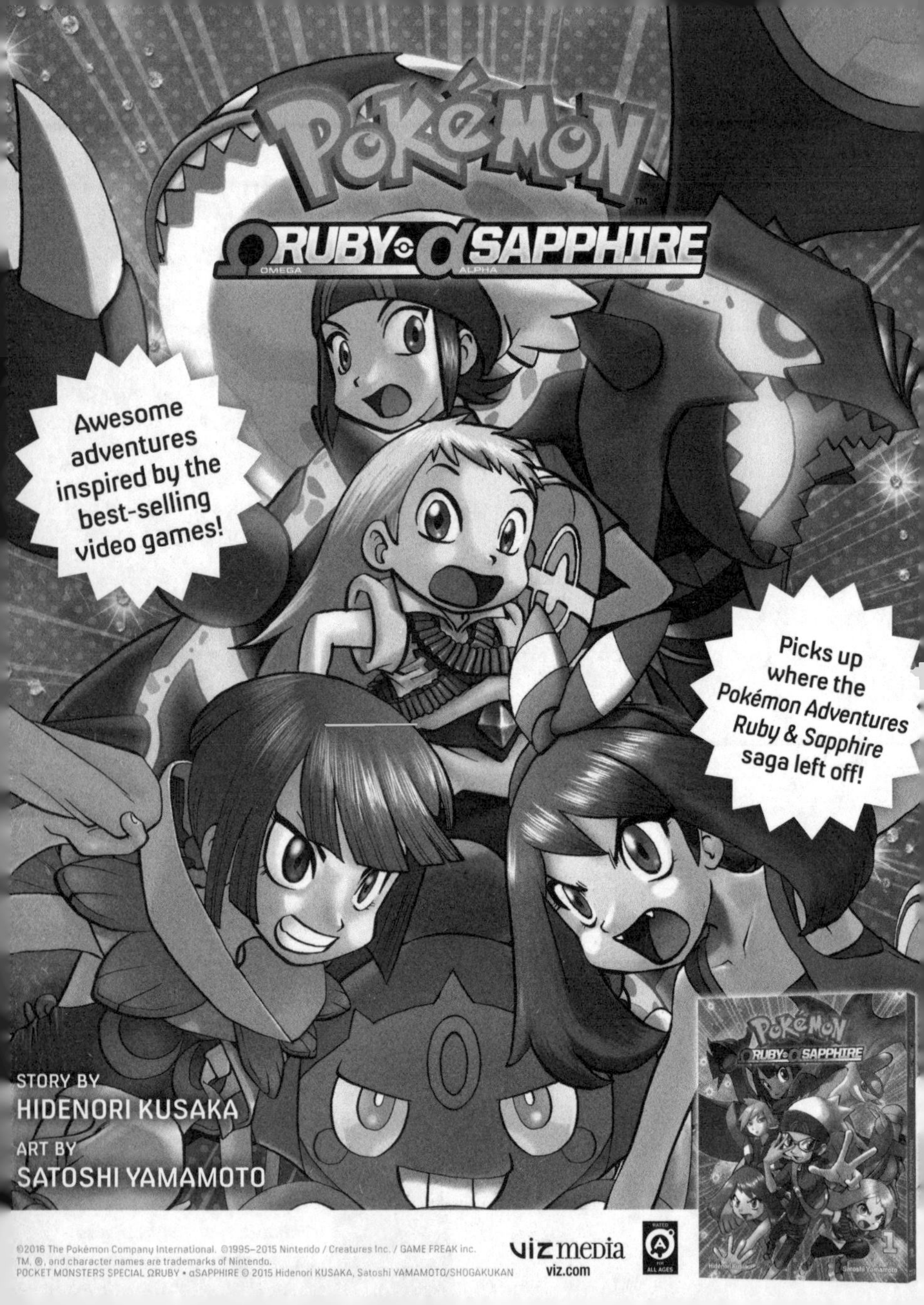
POKéMON
ΩRUBY • αSAPPHIRE
OMEGA ALPHA
Awesome adventures inspired by the best-selling video games!
Picks up where the Pokémon Adventures Ruby & Sapphire saga left off!
STORY BY
HIDENORI KUSAKA
ART BY
SATOSHI YAMAMOTO
©2016 The Pokémon Company International. ©1995–2015 Nintendo / Creatures Inc. / GAME FREAK inc.
TM, ®, and character names are trademarks of Nintendo.
POCKET MONSTERS SPECIAL ΩRUBY • αSAPPHIRE © 2015 Hidenori KUSAKA, Satoshi YAMAMOTO/SHOGAKUKAN
viz media
viz.com
RATED A FOR ALL AGES

2/22

THIS IS THE END OF THIS GRAPHIC NOVEL!

To properly enjoy this VIZ Media graphic novel, please turn it around and begin reading from right to left.

This book has been printed in the original Japanese format in order to preserve the orientation of the original artwork. Have fun with it!

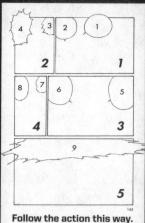

‹‹‹ READ THIS WAY!

Follow the action this way.